DANGEROUS SECRETS

H KRUEGER

Dangerous Secrets
Copyright © 2023 by HKrueger

All rights reserved. No part of this publication may be reproduced, distributed, or transmitted in any form or by any means, including photocopying, recording, or other electronic or mechanical methods, without the prior written permission of the author, except in the case of brief quotations embodied in critical reviews and certain other non-commercial uses permitted by copyright law.

ISBN
978-1-961250-09-3 (Paperback)
978-1-961250-10-9 (eBook)
978-1-961250-08-6 (Hardcover)

DANGEROUS SECRETS

Table of Contents

Chapter 1 1
Chapter 2 4
Chapter 3 8
Chapter 4 11
Chapter 5 15
Chapter 6 18
Chapter 7 21
Chapter 8 24
Chapter 9 28
Chapter 10 32
Chapter 11 37
Chapter 12 42
Chapter 13 47
Chapter 14 50
Chapter 15 56
Chapter 16 63
Chapter 17 68
Chapter 18 75
Chapter 19 79
Chapter 20 85

Chapter 21 89
Chapter 22 94
Chapter 23 98
Chapter 24 102
Chapter 25 106
Chapter 26 111
Chapter 27 117
Chapter 28 123
Chapter 29 128
Chapter 30 134
Chapter 31 138
Chapter 32 141

Chapter 1

Sam lay upon a large blanket on the snowy white sandy beach, his eyes closed, basking in solitude, dreaming of the past. Suddenly, a shadow comes over him. Opening his eyes slowly, the bright sun outlines the silhouette of a beautiful woman. She stands there, not saying a word.

The hint of a smile crosses her face. "Well, hello there. Were you sleeping?"

"No," Sam replies, shaking his head. "I was…. uhh... just resting." Their eyes meet and they gaze at one another silently, as if they know each other from another place or time.

The woman breaks the spell with, "May I join you?"

"Please do! I would enjoy the company," Sam quickly responds. He notices the reddish brown highlights in her hair as the sun shines down upon her.

Giving her his full attention, he stands up. The lady seems to take note of Sam's well-tanned and defined body. His hair has just the slightest curl giving his face an honest, gentle appearance. She looks at his 6'2" frame and gazes into his deep blue eyes. Extending his hand, Sam introduces himself.

"My name is Sam. What brings you to this part of the island?" As their fingers touch, a sudden unexplainable feeling overcomes them. The sensation is electrifying, stimulating and most intriguing.

Taking a deep breath, she says, "My name is… Dee. I was just walking along the beach, you know, some quiet time to myself. I saw you lying here and for some reason I was compelled to stop and say hello."

Sam feels mesmerized, transfixed by her dark, mysterious eyes that inaudibly scream of passion and hint of even more. Her body has curves that no man would ever tire of. "I'm very glad you did stop, Dee," he says.

She notices his smile as he tips his head down a bit, then glancing upward, he tells her, "You know... this *is* a private section of the island."

"Oh?" Dee coyly exclaims, "I really wasn't aware that I had walked that far. Do you think the owner will be upset?"

"No, " Sam quips, "I'm not upset at all."

She detects a trace of laughter in his voice. "What? You own this place?" she says, abruptly turning her attention to the shore.

"Oh, please…it's actually my pleasure to have you here…Really!" He rests his hand on her shoulder to reassure her that she is welcome.

Dee glances at his hand, then turns to look upon his face. For a moment she becomes lost in thought. "Uh…O.K," she stutters. "I really do need to be going, though, it was very nice meeting you, Sam."

"Wait!" he says in a panic. "Can we perhaps meet again, later this evening? Over drinks, maybe?"

Dee pleasantly replies, "We really haven't had any time to get to know each other so, yes, I think I would like that."

Anxiously, Sam continues. "I will meet you around five p.m. then. Umm, would the Casa Blanca restaurant be OK?"

Dee gleefully replies, "At that time and place, you shall see my face."

As she turns to walk away, she hears Sam say to her, "'Til later, then?"

"Yes, I'll be looking forward to it," Dee replies as she sashays off.

Sam studies her steady gliding motion across the sand. As he watches, his mind now races a million miles an hour as to who this lady is, where she comes from, and many more questions. Her image slowly fades into the distance. Sitting back down, Sam mentally replays the vision of her graceful walk and the sweet sound of her angelic voice.

He can't seem to get her out of his head as he reclines once again, and closes his eyes. An hour goes by when his cell phone rings. It's a reminder of his two o'clock meeting that afternoon. Sam decides he'll rest a bit longer before returning home to get dressed for the meeting. His dream takes him back to a time when his beloved wife was still alive. This dream was different, though, not like the others.

In this dream, there she stood before him, her hands tied, and only a simple sheet wrapped around her. Sam saw that she was standing on some sort of a board. She was looking at him, trying to speak. A terrified look was on her face as she worked at keeping her balance. Sam tried to get to her but no matter how hard he tried, he could not make his way to her. The more he tried, the further she would drift away. In the dream, Sam made a gallant leap for the board, knocking her into the water.

Now Sam finally reached her. Pulling the tape from her lips, she looked at Sam with sorrowful eyes as she tried to speak. Just as the first few words came out, Sam's cell phone went off, jarring him awake with a start. Beads of sweat ran from his brow as he suddenly felt a chill in the air.

Taking a deep breath, Sam tried to recall what she was trying to say to him in the dream. All he could make out was something about, "Please! Don't be…"

"Don't be what?" he asked himself. Looking down at his watch, he now saw that his time was short. Rushing home, he swiftly changed his clothes so he could get to the office on time…all the while, the vision of his late wife still haunting him.

Chapter 2

Upon arriving at the office, Sam is greeted by his secretary, Rachael. Rachael is a fine young woman, late 20's, full of life and always willing to do her best. She has a slender build with gorgeous cascading black hair. She is more than just Sam's secretary though as she is also his confidant and timekeeper.

Rachael hands him his messages as he walks past her saying Hello. Racheal remarks "Hello there Sir!" Sam then stops at the doorway and says to her "Please, hold my calls 'til the meeting is through." Rachael tells him no problem as he walks into his office and closes the door. Sam's mind is not on the meeting right now but still back on the beach. Thoughts of the new lady he met and the dream about his deceased wife weigh heavily upon his mind.

As Sam sits down to start checking his messages, he turns, taking a moment look out the window at the beachfront view. Relaxing back in his high back leather chair, thoughts of Dee start rushing through his mind like the ocean waves, one after another. Suddenly, the buzz of his intercom snaps him back to reality. The soft voice he now hears, tells him that it is two o'clock and all of his staff are in the conference room waiting. "Thank--you," he replies as he grabs his agenda and heads for the meeting.

Sam enters the boardroom, takes his seat at the head of the table and begins, "O.k., lets talk about the AMTRON buyout". "John, have they signed the contracts and deeds yet?" John looks up, "Well, not yet, they're being hesitant for some reason." Sam, not liking this little set back at all, takes a deep breath, "Well, just what the Hell is their problem, now? We've been going back and forth like this for too long. Those papers should have been signed last week, already. The fiscal year is about up and we NEED to get this done."

John replies, "I have a meeting with them at nine a.m. tomorrow and I'm sure I'll get this whole thing straightened out." Sam can hear the uneasiness in John's voice. Looking John straight in the eye, Sam sternly says, "That's not an answer, John! Now, WHAT is their concern?" John pauses for a moment looking around the room before answering. "They are just not seeming to like our offer and…."

Sam quickly interrupts, "Don't like our offer?! How about we just shut them down and take it for half the price at the auction?" Sam changes his attention to another board member. "Mike, how does our budget look if we raise our offer?"

Mike looks through his folder and tells Sam, "We can go another five million without a problem, but I gotta tell ya, it really isn't worth that much." "Let Me worry about what it's worth. I want that company." Sam replies emphatically.

Looking back at John, Sam says, "Tell ya what John, I'll go with you tomorrow and make sure they understand that this is my last offer. I want to see everything you have on this up-to-date and on my desk by five p.m. today. Also, Mike, I want the companies last two years of revenue reports and profit loss statements on my desk as well." Both men agree to have the reports ready. "Now lets get back to work, I have other matters to attend to." Sam then leaves the room.

As Sam goes back to his office, he closes his door a little harder than usual. Racheal knows something is not right, she softly knocks on the door, then opens it slowly. She enters with a puzzled look on her face asking if everything is OK or is there something she can do for him. Sam looks up from his desk "Why? What are you talking about?" A little more puzzled now, Racheal asks "Well, you don't usually slam your door. I just figured you might need something or at least an ear perhaps?"

"Naw, just one of those days I guess." Sam replies "I'll let you know when I need something." "OK fine." Racheal says as she turns to leave.

Sam sits and one again starts to relive the moments at the beach. "There is something very familiar about Dee but I just can't figure it." he thinks to himself. After about an hour of shuffling through papers and calling back messages, John walks into Sam's office. He has with him all the notes on the meetings up-to-date. As he places them on Sam's desk he remarks, "Here are the reports you requested."

Sam looks at John with out even going through the pile he just received on his desk. "John" he asks "Why are you seeming to be so nervous about this buyout? You've been with me from day one of this company. This is nothing new. Is there something you're not telling me?" "Just got a lot on my mind I guess. Maybe I need a vacation" John replies as he shakes his head a bit and manages a smile.

As John leaves Sam's office, Sam cannot shake the uneasy feeling about John being so nervousness over this deal. As he looks through the papers hoping to find an answer, his mind starts to wander. He starts thinking again about the little disturbing dream from earlier. As he looks to one side, he is suddenly drawn to a picture on his desk. It's a picture of a woman of whom he once loved so dearly. Her name was Robin, the one true love of his life.

Robin was the reason for Sam's push and fervent drive against AMTRON. Sitting back in his chair and looking out at the ocean, he recalls only too well, just a few years back, a most memorable, yet horrifying 4th of July......He and his beautiful wife were sitting on their boat, just off shore, watching the display of fireworks. He recalls how Robin looked that day. Her fine Purple shorts and tank top, that smile that he could look at for hours on end. The burst of colors from the fire works display seemed to dance in her eyes and lit up her soft brown hair.

Others were with them that night, everyone laughing and having a great time. The fire works display was given by the very same company that he was now trying to buyout. After the show was over, the boat headed back for dock. All his guests left, saying their goodbyes. After the last one left. Sam turned to Robin. Looking at her standing there, remembering the look on her face as she smile and they embraced.

Arm in arm they left the boat and walked to the car parked at dock side. Robin stopped and exclaimed "Dang it! I left my purse on the boat. Would you be a dear and go get it for me?" Sam of course agreed and went quickly into the boat to retrieve what his wife had left.

Humming all the way into the cabin, his gleeful mood was cut short by a loud and very close explosion. There was burst of light, filling the cabin as it rocked in the water. Sam ran up the short steps to the deck. There, to his horror, he saw what was left of his car. Robin's body laid motionless about 50 feet away. He yelled her name as he ran to her. Taking her into his arms, Robin looked up slowly taking a slow forced breath. All she could manage to say was "I…. Please.." Then exhaling slowly the rest of her breath, Robin fell limp in his arms.

Sam screamed in remorse looking up at the night sky. People were starting to gather now to see what had happened. The police found remains of a rocket from the display that night, in the back seat of what was left of Sam's car. The investigation however was inconclusive and as to being deliberate or accident. The final ruling in the report was listed as accidental. Sam was told that apparently it didn't go off until after it had fallen into the car.

Sam vowed revenge, however his efforts were futile as the case was dismissed. He could not prove that this came from AMTRON's display. Sam however would not stop there or let this matter drop. Due to the bad publicity though aimed at AMTRON, the Government pulled the contract that AMTRON and Sam's company shared. Now, with the entire contract going to Sam's company, it was only a matter of time before AMTRON would have to fold.

Sam saw his chance to make them pay for their misdeed as soon as he learned of the pending financial problems of the other company. Sam knew he had to buy them out. He had to be the one to shut that place down forever. The bitter memories were breaking Sam's heart once more as the anger was building inside. Looking down at his desk, he continues once more reading the folder John left for him.

Chapter 3

Sam glances at the clock on the wall, it is almost 4 o'clock. Getting up from his chair, Sam stretches, then walks out of his office, stopping at Rachael's desk. He tells her that he is leaving for the day and she might as well go too. "Are you sure?" she asks. "I don't mind waiting if you need me to do so." Sam smiles and looks at her. "No, No, you just go ahead, you work late enough as it is. So, you have a good evening and I'll see you in the morning." Sam turns to leave. "O.K. then, goodnight, Sir!" She says as he walks out. "Goodnight." Sam replies.

As Sam drove home, the anticipation of seeing Dee grows inside. He can think of nothing else as he drives up to his large cobblestone estate with all the wealthy amenities, tennis court, hot tub, Olympic size swimming pool and the most beautiful landscape ever. Parking his car, he gets out and walks up the steps to the front door. Entering, he finds the housekeeper listening to her radio and dancing while she dusts. Shaking his head with a smile, Sam walks up to his room to shower and change his clothes.

As Sam comes back down the stairs, he is seen by the house keeper, Shannon. Shannon has been with Sam since the very first day he and his wife bought the house. It was as if she had come with it. Shannon is in her early 30's, intelligent and energetic. Her 5'4" frame that is in excellent shape is highlighted by her natural dark complexion. She has Jet Black hair past her shoulders and the most beautiful greenish blue eyes. All this allows Shannon to get away with being such a smart-ass.

As he starts to tell her about his date tonight, she notices the subtle glow upon his face. She just smiles and tells him to have a good time. Walking out the back door to the garage, Sam suddenly feels a chill in the air. He stops and out of the corner of his eye, he swears he saw someone standing in the background along side of the garage. As quickly as the image appeared, it vanished.

Shaking it off as just nerves and tension from work, Sam gets into his car and off he goes to meet with Dee. As he arrives, Sam stops in front of the restaurant. The Valet quickly comes over and Sam gets out, allowing the valet to park the car. As Sam stands there, he looks around for Dee, but she is no where in sight as of yet. He starts to wonder if this mystery lady is going to show or not. Soon, he notices a car pull up and Dee steps out from the passenger's side. He see's her lean back into the car and can faintly hear her say, "See you later back at the house" to the person inside the car.

Sam just stood there, wondering who this other person was. Dee waited for the car to drive off before she walked up to the restaurant entrance. Sam's heart skips a beat as he watches her walk toward him, as if she was floating on a cloud.

He admires her elegant poise and fashionable clothing. Dee wore a black chiffon skirt that flowed with every step. Raising his view, he gazes upon her white, sleeveless tie front blouse. Sam can hardly speak at this point.

With a smile on her face, Dee speaks, "Hello, I hope you didn't have to wait long" "Nope! Just got here myself Darlin'!" Sam replies as he reaches out to take her hand, giving it a gentle kiss. "You look very nice tonight!" He tells her. "Oh!?, Like I didn't look good before?" Dee says teasingly. "Well, NO! I mean….Uh " Sam fumbles for the right words.

Dee puts her hand on his shoulder gently, trying to hold back the laughter she says, "Relax, I was just teasing with you." Sam shook his a little with a smile of relief as they now entered the restaurant. Entering, they walked to the lounge area. They were greeted by the Maitre D', who immediately recognizes Sam. "Good evening Mr. Katz! Would you like a table on the terrace tonight?" He asks. Sam looks at Dee and sees the high brow smile on her face. Turning to the Maitre D' he tells him that would be fine.

Sam and Dee both feel the excitement in the air, along with a very relaxing sense of being together. The Maitre D' holds the chair for Dee. She hesitates in sitting and says, "I need to freshen up a bit. I'll be right back, please excuse me." She walks off while Sam sits to looks over the menu. First, he orders a drink for them both. Upon Dee's return, Sam helps her get seated.

She notices, sitting in front of her, a Strawberry Daiquiri. With a big smile Dee utters "Hmmm... My favorite. How did you know?" Sam looks at her and says, "Well, a Daiquiri IS the drink of beauty. So I felt that would be a good choice for you"

Dee just sits back in her seat, taking a deep breath she tells Sam, "Well you keep this up and its going to be an interesting evening for sure!" As she takes a sip, Sam begins to wonder, just what is it about her that seems so very familiar? He starts with casual conversation, "I've never seen you around here before, where are you from?" Dee looks up from her drink and tells him, "I'm from Europe, I'm out here on sort of a getaway type vacation. Which is very unusual for me cuz I really don't go anywhere. And how about you? Do you actually live out here on this Island?" "Well" Sam says, "I actually live here and in Dallas."

Noticing no accent, Sam now asks, "So, where were you born then?" Dee smiled a she replied, "I was actually born and raised in Houston Texas. I moved to Europe a few years ago." Thinking for a moment, Sam remarks, "Well then, I'm surprised I haven't met you before this since we almost grew up together. I was bread in them parts myself." Sam laughs. After a few moments of banter, the waiter approaches. Sam let Dee order first and then it was his turn. Sam asked for a bottle of their best wine to go with their dinner.

As they wait, they drift with the mood of the soft music playing in the background. The flicker of the lit candles on their table, dances in their eyes. They are transfixed upon each other as they talk. Before they knew it, the meal arrives. Sam waits to for Dee to take a bit first and make sure it is to her liking. "So, how is your dinner, My Dear?" Sam asks.

Dee looks up at Sam replying, "It's very tasty in deed." They both continued to eat, asking one question after another. Dee's questions though, seemed to be more Company Based issues about Amtron. Sam was not sure why she was so inquisitive, but didn't mind talking about anything at all with her. Sam was quite taken by just sound of her voice.

Chapter 4

Upon finishing dinner, They sit for a moment or two and then Sam stands up. He walks around to Dee and reaches out his hand, asking, "May I have this Dance?" "What? After eating all this you want what?" Dee looks up but can't keep a straight face. Sam was confused a bit for a second. But when Dee broke out laughing he felt a sigh of relief come over him. "I would love to Sir!" Dee finally says. Sam takes her hand and leads her to the dance floor. The music consumes them both as they find themselves close in each others arms.

Not a word is spoken while they glide around like they were dancing on air. After a few songs, they return to their table. "So, have you any room for dessert?" Sam asks. "Well I really shouldn't ya know" Dee quickly replies "...but... Do they have cheese cake?" A child like little grin is showing on her face. Quickly, Sam motions for the waiter.

As Sam orders, Dee pipes up and asks "Can I have mine with strawberries on it?" "Certainly Ma'am," is the reply. After a few moments, the dessert arrives. Emotions and feelings tonight were running a little on the high side for each of them. So they were both very quiet as they finish their dessert. Afraid to say what they are really thinking of for fear it may just scare off the other.

Sam finally breaks the silence and asks if she would like to do some more dancing. "I would love to but I can't tonight. I really do need to get home. Can we go some other night?" She asks with a smile. "No! No! No! Its tonight or forget it lady!" Dee looks very surprised at him. Sam then adds "Wish I had a camera for the look on your face right now." Then starts to laugh.

He could tell Dee didn't think is was all that funny. "OK. I'm sorry. Of course we can go again" he added. They exchange numbers and get up from the table. As they walked to the door, Sam stops for a moment, telling her he will be right back. Dee watches as he heads off to the restroom. As Dee continues on and stands in the front waiting area. Dee looks out the window that's on the front door and notices a car pull up. Quickly, she walks out to the car and tells the driver to leave. The car drove off as Sam was just staring to step outside to see if she had gone yet or waited for him.

Sam walks over to her where she stood on the sidewalk. Before he gets to ask why she is waiting outside instead of inside, Dee tells Sam, "You don't know how long it's been since I've laughed and had such a wonderful time. Thank-You very much" Sam smiles very big and replies, "Honestly, the pleasure was all mine Darlin'. It's been a long time for me as well. Are you expecting a ride or can I take you home?"

Dee thinks for just a second, to come up with a good story, She didn't want Sam to know she was really hoping he would ask to give her a ride home. "Well, I was going to call for a ride but since you offered, I would love to ride you... I mean with you!" she then sprouted the biggest smile you ever saw. "But only if its NOT out of your way," she adds." "It would never be out of my way if it's for you," replies Sam, looking deep into her eyes.

An excitement is felt deep down as they wait for the valet to bring around Sam's car. A beautiful Laser red convertible Mustang GT pulls up, Dee's eyes open wide. Sam opens the door and helps her in as the valet gets out of the other side. Sam walks around, tips the valet and gets in. Feeling the soft leather seats, Dee says, "Ya know, I don't seem to remember exactly where I live. We may have to drive around a bit till we find it". Sam notices the subtle coy smile on her face. "Well, O.K. then which way do we start?" Pointing, Dee says, "Just go that way. This island can't be that big. We should find it eventually" So off they drove.

Sam turns on the radio, asking what she would like to listen to. She picks a soft rock station then sits back to enjoy the ride. With the top down, the bright stars shine into the car as the breeze blows through her hair.

Sam notices and says, "Ya know, I've never given an Angel a ride before" Looking over at Sam, she smiles and takes his hand, squeezing it gently. Its not too long before he pulls up to her front door.

Sam quickly gets out and comes around to open the car door for her to get out. Taking her hand, he helps her, then walks her up to the house. Looking at her, he says, "So this is your house Huh?" Dee just smiles and tells him, "Actually it belongs to some friends of mine. They're letting me stay here for a while" Sam, now realized the person in the car must have been one of the friends.

Putting his hands on her sides, Sam says, "Oh! Well, I'm glad you had a good time tonight. I wasn't sure how it was going to turn out. I haven't done anything like this for quite some time." Dee answers him with "The night was wonderful and I'm very much looking forward to more dancing."

Sam's heart was now beating a little faster as he asked, "So, I'll call you in the morning then O.K.? And we'll set a time?" Dee tilts her head slightly, looking up at Sam. "Sure! But I have some things to do in the morning, I'm free for in the afternoon though, so you can call me then." Sam agrees and slowly leans in for a good night kiss. The moon is shining, the wind gently blows, their lips touch for the first time.

To Sam, nothing else exists at this moment. Dee also feels something stir inside, but it was not something she thought would happen. Sam pulls back, looks into her eyes and then gives her a hug, telling her Good Night. As he walks to his car, Sam stops at the door to look back for a moment before getting in. He watches as she enters the house and slowly closes the door. Sam now gets into his car and drives off down the dark road with the radio playing.

Meanwhile, Dee is still standing just inside of her door, leaning against it, thinking of Sam. After a few moments, she pushes off of the door and walks to her room to go to bed. Dreams of Sam and the events of the evening start to go through her mind.

Sam too is playing the night over in his mind as he drives. The music from his radio fades as he remembers Dee's voice and her laugh, remembering how sweet she sounds. Memories then flashed in his mind of things that were not from tonight, but from a time not to long ago. Things that were so similar to tonight's events, yet not the same at all. Images of his late wife, of how they would dance laughing. This was all too much like tonight with Dee. All the way home Sam thought about this.

Tired, Sam finally arrives at his house and pulls into the garage. Quietly he walks up to the house and turns off the alarm so he can enter. Closing the door behind him, the alarm is resets as he finds his way up the stairs and to his bed. Undressing quickly, Sam then slipped under his covers to drift off and sleep.

Chapter 5

Sam is awakened by the music from his radio early the next morning. However, he does not wish to get up and put an end to the dream he is having of Dee. Slowly and reluctantly though, he drags himself out of bed and climbs into the shower. Once the water hit his face, Sam's mind starts to clear and he reflects on last night's events. Suddenly he is snapped back into the present when he hears the voice of his housekeeper, Shannon. She yells up to Sam saying " Unless you are going to start that DIET you've been talking about for the past few years, you should be down here eating breakfast already!"

Sam just smiles and tells her he'll be down in a minute. Finishing up, he gets dressed and heads downstairs. The smell of fresh bacon fills the air as he takes a deep breath. "What's the matter? Out of breath already?" Shannon says with a little chuckle. "No, not quite, just really hungry today and your cooking smells really good" Sam replies. Sitting down at the table, he picks up the paper and starts to read while he drinks the coffee Shannon has prepared for him, "Gee, got in a little LATE last night, huh? Surprised you're this awake, today" Shannon said to Sam.

Looking up from his paper Sam replied "Darn! Did I forget to clear that with you again?" Sam chuckles. "WHAT was I thinking? Coming and going at all hours of the day and night. It's like I OWN the place or something," Sam says now with a little laugh. "Just doing my job here and watching over things " Shannon says with a big smile. "Well, I ain't paying you anything extra for overtime so you don't have to watch THAT closely" Sam tells her jokingly. "PAY!?... There's a Paycheck for doing all of this?" Shannon says with a raised eyebrow and a smile. "Well, there WAS!" He retorts, trying to keep a straight face.

Shannon just shakes her head and continues cooking. Breakfast is severed and Sam eats quickly. He wants to get to the office early today and check on the reports that should already be on his desk. Grabbing his briefcase, he tells Shannon good-bye and heads off to the office.

Arriving early, he finds Rachael is not in yet. Going into his office, Sam looks at his desk to see if the report is there, per his request. Sure enough it is. Sitting down, he picks the report up and reads through it. The revenue report seems complete enough, the figures show that the Amtron Company needs to either sell or go bankrupt. In the folder from John, Sam finds his report very hard to follow. He calls John into his office to get an explanation of this confusing report.

When John arrives, Sam is not sure which question to ask him first. Scanning the first page he begins, "Now John, I would like you to explain to me exactly what is meant by this memo from Amtron regarding side shares not accounted for in the original bid?" "Well," John starts to explain, "There were some shares of the company that were set aside and used for a silent backer a few years ago. They wouldn't tell me who they belonged to but assured me it would not be a problem for the sale."

John seemed very uneasy while waiting for Sam's reaction. "You know, something just isn't right about this whole damn thing. Why didn't you come to me with this information when you found out about it? John, you've been with me for many years and I've never questioned your decisions or felt the need to follow up on you for anything. Why is this buyout becoming such a problem and mystery? Hell, I'm waiting for that lady from Murder She Wrote to come walking in here any minute now." Sam seems to have an irritated tone in his voice as he speaks to John.

John donned a very concerned, almost worried look upon his face as he says, "Sam, there really is NOTHING to worry about. If I thought it would have been a problem then I would have told you right away. After all these years, why are you second guessing me, NOW?" John takes a deep breath and looks straight at Sam. Sam says, "I suppose your right,

Buddy. I just want this company so bad, perhaps I'm just blowing things out of proportion. Well, it's almost time to leave for the meeting today. I do have a few calls to make first. So, go get your stuff and I should be ready to go by then."

John agrees and turns to leave. As the door closes, Sam begins to think of all the things he would REALLY like to say at that meeting with Amtron. Moments later, he reaches for his wallet to pull out a phone number, remembering his promise to Dee. He calls the number to schedule their lunch date. As the line rings, he pictures her lovely face and what she wore last night.

A male voice utters from the other end of the line, "Hello?" Perhaps this was who Dee had drop her off last night for their dinner date, Sam thought to himself. Sam asked for Dee and was surprised to hear, "I'm sorry Pal but there's no Dee at this number." Sam quickly looked at the number again and said it to the man on the phone. "Well, yes you have the right number, but I've never heard of anyone named Dee. Sounds like you may have had a little joke played on you." the unknown voice replied.

"Well, sorry to have bothered you." Sam said as he hung up the phone wondering WHY she would have given him a wrong number. After all, she was the one who wrote it down and gave it to him, so it's not like he wrote it down wrong. A bit confused now, Sam continues with work. As he goes over last minute notes before the meeting, John returns. "Ready to go?" he asks. Sam looks up quickly and nods. Gathering his papers and thoughts, he and John leave the office.

Sam stopped at the desk first though and lets Racheal know that there may be a lady calling for him named Dee. If she calls, Rachael is to page Sam right away with a call back number. Rachael writes down his instructions and then answers the phone that has just started to ring. Sam freezes in his tracks as he hears, "I'm sorry Sir, you just missed him….." She waves Sam on to just leave, knowing he was hoping it would have been Dee calling. Disappointed, Sam leaves with John for the meeting.

Chapter 6

Meanwhile, Dee is just now waking up. The phone ringing caused her to stir. Sitting up in her bed, she yells from her room, "Who was on the phone this early in the morning?" hoping to hear that a guy named Sam was calling for her. She hears NO reply. Getting out of bed and putting on her robe, She walks out of her bedroom and down the hall to the kitchen. There she sees Adam, sitting at the table drinking his coffee.

While he is looking out the window, she walks up to him and says, "Hey, Adam! Aren't you awake? Who was on the phone?" "Oh just a wrong number. Some guy looking for a lady named Dee." Adam replied, noticing the guilty look on her face, "You didn't tell him who you are, did you? Did you tell him your name was Dee? You should have told me. Now the guy is going think you were just messing with him. You need to come up with some good story now, unless you plan to really tell him what's going on." Adam told her.

Looking a little puzzled as to what to do, she thought hard for a moment before answering. "I know, I know. One thing lead to another and I forgot all about the other name I gave him. It's just that he is not what I expected at all. I sort of just got wrapped up in the moment. My name was not a key issue last night. When I gave him this number, I simply forgot I didn't use my real name. Don't worry, I'll take care of it." She says and then turns to leave the room.

Going back to the bedroom, she goes straight to the shower. While showering, she thinks of what she will be telling Sam. Finishing her shower, she turns off the water and hears a song on the radio. The song takes her back to last night with Sam. Day dreaming now of what a wonderful time she had and how they danced to this song, many other things went through her mind as well while she got ready for the day.

Thinking of a good story to tell Sam, she decided to give him a call. "Hello, H.K. Industries, how may I help you?" She heard the voice say. "Uh Yes, I'm trying to reach Mr. Katz Please?" Dee said. Sam's phone rings and Rachael answers. "Mr. Katz office, may I help you?" A little nervously Dee says, "Yes, hello, how are you? Is Sam there by chance?" "He's on his way to a meeting right now. May I take a message or help you with something?" Rachael says.

"Well, we were supposed to meet today for lunch and…" "Is this Dee?" Rachael interjects. "Yes it is." Dee replies, wondering what Sam has told her. "He told me to page him if you should call. What is the number for him to return your call?" asked Rachael. Dee calls out the number, informing Rachael that she will be at that number all morning. Rachael closes the conversation with pleasantries and a farewell. She then immediately pages Sam.

At the meeting, Sam is sitting at the one end of the table and Mr. William P. Hornsby,(the owner of Amtron Inc.) at the other end. William, a.k.a. Wild Bill, infamously known as one of the best word game players in the business, is a man in his mid 40's. Bill has a light mix of gray in his hair and slightly over weight. He has the reputation of being a true cold-hearted businessman with a passion for big money. Being only 5' 10" he comes at you like he was 8 feet tall. Sam knows all to well of "Wild Bill's" reputation.

Nonetheless, Sam loves knowing that Bill does not have the upper hand here and doesn't believe that Bill will turn him down. After the pleasantries and formalities of the meeting are done, Sam starts in "O.K. now, let me get this straight Bill, you think your company is still worth something? I'm doing you a favor offering this much. I've seen the financial reports and I've done my homework. Your assets and liabilities are well under the amount I am offering, not to mention, you have no REAL Capitol to speak of. WHY are you hanging on? There are no other offers on table this high and no one else is left in the bidding because they are not willing to go as high. So what's your angle? What the Hell are you looking for!?"

Sam looks square into Bill's icy cold eyes as he awaits an answer. "Well" Bill replies, "To tell you the truth, Sam. Your offer is high, yes, and that's why I'm a bit hesitant about selling it to you. If you are willing to offer this much, then, there must be something that you see that no else does. I'm beginning to wonder if I should try one more time, just to see if I can find out what is it that you REALLY want. Hmmm, what shall I do!???" Bill replies with a tone in his voice that tells Sam more than Bill's words.

Sam knows now there is something going on here, making the inner desire to put this guy out of business, grow even more. But, what is it that Bill is waiting for? Why is he playing this game when all the reports clearly display that this company is heading into bankruptcy? These are the things that course through Sam's mind while he listens to Bill talk.

Sam responds as he slowly rises from his chair. It's a last stand so to speak, a power play against a man that Sam sees only as the enemy and nothing more. "Look! This is the offer, this is the deal, it will only be good until the close of business today. Call my office when you decide. We have been here for an hour hashing this out. It's time for you to sign or I'll take my chances at the Bank Auction after you loose everything! Take it or leave it, I'll be waiting to hear from you. In the end I will own this building, this company and whatever else is left." Sam uses a cocky tone and looks coldly back at Bill.

Bill replies as if Sam's tactics had no real effect, "Well, I will certainly think about it and get back to you later". Sam was about to respond just as his pager went off. Looking down, Sam views the message on his pager, "Dee Called. 555-7379 RE: lunch?) Taking a deep breath, Sam looks up and says, "Well, as I've stated, I'll be waiting to hear from you, today." His tone seemed to leave an echo in the room. Sam says Good-bye and exits Bill's office with John.

Thinking about the number on his pager, he checks it with the one in his wallet from the other night just before he gets in his car. "Strange" he thought to himself, "It's the same one as from last night." As Sam drives back to his office, he can't wait to call her and find the answer to this number game. As he parks his car, he notices a car, suddenly racing off from in front of his building. "Wonder where they're going so fast? Hope there's not a problem. I got enough crapp going on right now!" Sam thought to himself, as he continues on now, going up to his office.

Chapter 7

Rachael greets Sam as he walks in, handing him a few messages. Two of them are from Dee. "Seems like you made quite an impression on the young lady last night" Rachael says with an inquisitive tone. "Yes, I thought so too. You know, there's something about her that I just can't quite put my finger on," Sam murmurs, almost to himself, as he walks into his office. Now sitting at his desk, he picks up the phone and dials the number. While the line is connecting, Sam leans back and stares out his window. Sam notices the car he had seen earlier now parked outside.

As he starts to wonder, a voice answers the line, it was a male voice again. This time however, it was a recording. "Hello! You have just about reached me. Please leave a message and I'll see if I can reach YOU!" A simple message was all Sam left "Well, this is me. Give me a call, please" just as soon as he hung up, he heard Rachael say on the intercom "You have a call on line 3, It's a Ms. Taylor, Do want to take it or shall I take a message?" "Send it in, thank you," Sam said raising a brow and wondering who it was.

Sam answered the line when it rang in. In a very Professional sounding Hello, he heard the voice he had been waiting for. "Well, hello there Sam! Miss Me!?" It was Dee and she had the sound of excitement in her voice. "Why, was I supposed to?" Sam replied with a noticeable laugh, "Let's see now, you are the Huh, mystery woman I met yesterday right? I gotta tell you, you are hard to get hold of. I thought I was always busy. I tried your number but I guess I miss read your handwriting when I called you this morning."

Dee interrupted quickly, "Sorry about that. When I told you my name on the beach, I wasn't exactly honest with you." Sam listened as she explained to him that she was very nervous when she talked to him, wasn't sure if she should give her real name. It's a girl thing she explain. "It's like a protection so guys can't track me down real easy. I was going to tell you last night after dinner but I was so wrapped up in the evening I completely forgot. My real name is Kathy, will you forgive me?" She said with sincerity.

Sam was quiet for a moment, gathering his thoughts, he then replied "Yes, I can see why such an attractive lady would want to be careful. Is there anything else you would like to tell me about?" Sam asked, being rather curious at this point. "Nothing that I can think of, Why?" Kathy said. "Well, it's just that I don't remember giving you the number here at work." Kathy thought quickly and responded "Well, you told me on the beach you owned that part of it, so I,... did some checking of my own. You WERE called by your last name at dinner also you know. So I put two and two together and let my fingers do the walking….. are you, upset with me?" She asks.

After a momentary pause, Sam replies "Hmmmm, let me see. Tell you what, if you have lunch with me all is forgiven." Kathy hears the chuckle in his voice and quickly accepts, saying, "You drive a hard bargain there, Sir! But, I will gladly accept your terms!" Kathy laughs. They set the time and place to meet, then said their good-byes before hanging up. Just as Sam puts down the receiver, he hears a car racing off outside.

Looking out his window, Sam notices the vehicle he had seen earlier sitting out there, is now gone. Shaking his head slightly, Sam dismisses it as just a coincidence. Getting back to work now, Rachael walks into his office, placing some files on his desk, she remarks, "If you don't mind me asking. Who was that on the phone? Was it Dee?" looking at Sam with an inquisitive stance. "Yes and no," Sam replies, "Apparently, I was given a made up name in the beginning, she said it was a protection thing." Rachael then adds "Well, us girls gotta watch out you know for smooth talkers like you."

Rachael notices that Sam is not smiling from what she said. Taking a step closer she touches his shoulder. "Are you O.K.? Normally, you would have had a come back. What's up?" Rachael says with great concern. Sam looks up and says, "You always seem to know when things aren't right with me. There is something nagging away at me about her, but I just can't quite figure it out." Sam takes a deep breath, relieving some of the tension that is building up inside him.

Sam then remarks, "I know I have heard her voice before, but where? It's as if I've known her from somewhere or something," "Look," Rachael says "I wasn't going to tell you this but, when she called, my heart took a little skip too. She really sounds just like… Well, and I don't want to stir up anything but… She sounds a lot like your wife did."

Rachael looks at Sam, noticing his cold look upon his face. In a soft tone Sam tells her "You know my wife has been gone for a few years now and I really don't want to think that the reason I'm attracted to this lady is because she reminds me of HER". Realizing his tone, Sam quickly added. "I'm sorry, I… I didn't mean to snap at you like that. Perhaps you are right. But I know there is more to my interest than just a voice from the past. Her real name is Kathy. At least that's what it is for today." Sam says, looking confused.

Rachael looks at him, giving assurance that she understands what he is trying to say and wishing she had never made that comment to him now. Rachael returns out front to her desk and thinks to herself, "Sure am glad I didn't also say I thought about his wife Robin was because "Taylor" was Robin's maiden name. She begins to type and free her mind of her boss's personal issues.

Sam leans back in his big chair for what he thought was just a moment. Quickly however, he found himself once again reliving the night he lost more than a wife. There she was, laying with in his arms, a tear running down her face as she looked at him. She struggled with the words, "Please, forgive me, I…" once again though, even though he had relived this moment so many times in his mind, he could not make out what she was trying to tell him. Suddenly, Sam snaps out of his dream as quickly as he had entered. Realizing he only has about 15 minutes till he is to with Kathy, Sam gets up and walks over to Rachael. He tells her about his lunch plans and that he would be coming back.

Chapter 8

Sam walks out to his car and drives off with a million questions on his mind about Kathy. He wants to know so much that he starts to laugh a little, thinking to himself that he should have made a list before he left. Sam has the top down on his car as he enjoys the breeze and the beckoning of the shore heard in the distance. A white car pulls up alongside, lingering just a bit, then speeds off ahead. Realizing this is the same car that was parked outside earlier, Sam speeds up, trying to see the driver or its possible passenger. However, because of the tinted windows, Sam could see nothing at all. An uneasy feeling came over Sam causing him to slow back down and not entice the other car to a show down right now.
Suddenly, the car jettisons a left turn on the green light with no signal or warning. Sam slowly drives through the intersection, watching the other car as it continues down the road. Sam looks ahead again at where he is going, wondering what is going on. Approaching the meeting place, a quaint little Caecilian-style restaurant, he sees Kathy, waiting for him at a table out on the porch. Kathy did not notice him yet, so after he parks, Sam makes walks over to a flower vendor on the sidewalk. Buying a single white rose, he hides it behind his back as he walks up to the restaurant.

    Kathy was quite surprised when Sam walked up behind her. Kathy jumps slightly, then turns around to face him. Kathy's wide eyes and beaming smile, told Sam his little surprise was well received. She says, as she inhales the fresh scent of the rose, "HELLO!! It's so beautiful, Thankyou!" Sam then whispers into her ear "The way I see it, I want to show this rose what TRUE beauty really is." Kathy is left speechless and simply sighs as she sits back down.

Sam walks around and sits across from her, then asks about how her day is going. The waitress comes over after a few minutes and asks if they are ready to order. After Sam and Kathy place their order and the waitress is walking away, Kathy jests, "Gee, that lady acted as if she didn't even know you. Not like the restaurant we were at last night. Could it be, you don't know everyone on this Island?" "Hmm, she must be new!" Kathy laughs as Sam quickly and wittingly retorts, "Yes, I will make note of that and come back later."

Kathy notices after a few moments that Sam is looking right at her while she speaks, yet has a look on his face like he's a million miles away. Thinking quickly, Kathy vers off in mid sentence and says, "I also have three breasts and my skin is actually a light green around my ass!" With both eyebrows a bit raised she looks at him and waits for an answer. "Oh, I see. Wait! What did you say?" Sam replied looking a bit embarrassed. Kathy proceeded, "I see how you are going to be, ask me something and then not listen. Tell ya what..."

Quickly Sam interrupts "It's just that, although I am really trying to listen to what you are saying, I am totally mesmerized by your beautiful green eyes." "Well" Kathy says, "I'll have to keep my eye on you." She then reaches across the table for his hand, gently squeezing his fingers. The food arrives now and so they begin to enjoy their meal.

Looking up from his plate, Sam notices directly behind Kathy, on the other side of the street, is the white car again. This time, as it slowly drives by, Sam exclaims "That's it!" "What!? Am I eating with the wrong fork or something?" Kathy says being more than a little startled. Kathy looks in the same direction as Sam and asks what he is looking at. "Nothing out of the ordinary to me." Kathy remarks.

Sam tells her about the car he just saw and how it keeps showing up all day where ever he is at. "The Darn thing seems to be following me everywhere and it's getting on my nerves!" I'm going to find out just who owns that car and why they are so interested in me" Sam tells her with a tone of conviction. Kathy quickly tries to make light of it to get his mind on something else. "Well, let's just eat for now and enjoy this warm sunny day. Please don't let it bother you. I'm sure it's nothing at all."

Kathy continues, trying to distract Sam from stressing. "Look, I know, just close your eyes for a moment and take a deep breath." As Sam does this, Kathy quietly gets up and moves close. Bending down, she gives Sam a kiss. He takes a quick little breath as he feels her lips touch his. He is now only thinking and feeling about what is happening at this moment. Standing straight, Kathy says, "Now, if THAT doesn't ease your mind, I'm going home... Well, is there any car on your mind?" Sam immediately responds, "Car? What car???" as he breaths slowly and relaxes.

Returning to their meals, he asks her what she does for a living. "I'm a Freelance Art Designer." She tells him. "I travel all over the place. I Love doing it even though there ARE times when the pay kinda sucks, if you know what I mean. But, I'm working on establishing an actual business and I thought I would like to do that on an Island. Give it that "carefree and exotic" type feeling to help attract people" She looks deeply into his eyes. Sam says back to her, "Sounds like we may have some business to talk about later. That is, IF you would like any help setting this up." As he shows a big smile.

"Dang, there you go again. Do you turn all your lunch dates into business? So you want to umm, check my ASSets? Perhaps my Portfolio too?" Sam notices she is trying not to smile making this comment. "Well, I can't think of anyone that would make a prettier Business partner that's for sure!" Sam replies. Kathy is finding herself at a loss for words for the first time since she met Sam.

Kathy finds herself very touched at this point, suddenly feeling as though she is getting way more than she had bargained for. Sam then asks her if she is free this weekend. Thinking quickly, trying to avoid what she is really thinking, she tells him, "Well, I do usually charge, but since you are such pleasant company, I'll be free for you." Sam is not quite sure how to respond. He has never really come up against a lady like this, one that can throw it back at him so well. Only Shannon has ever been able to do that.

Kathy see's he is at a loss and says, "What did you have in mind?" "Well," Sam says, finally finding his tongue. "I would like to know if you would take a little trip with me. We could get to know each other better, no interruptions, just you and I. What do you say?" Sam awaits her answer.

"Let me check what's going on and I'll call you later this evening to let you know, O.K? I really would like to go," Kathy tells Sam with a little excitement in her voice as she talks.

Sam too is filled with a bit of excitement, he has not dated since the accident years ago. Sam wonders if he will even know how to act anymore on a date. As the two get up to depart, they stop at the front entrance. He tells her he'll be waiting for her call. A soft tender kiss is given. Kathy then tells him, "I WILL be calling". Sam then turns to pay the check.

When he turns back around, he notices Kathy did not wait for him. He looks out side, to see if he can spot her. Soon, he notices she is all the way over across the street. Puzzled as to why she did not wait, Sam just watched her as she walked so gracefully, disappearing into the rows of cars that were parked over there. The Cashier now gets his attention to give him his change. The break in his watching, was enough to not allow Sam to see the white car again, now pull out of the Parking lot that Kathy just entered.

As Sam gets into his car to head back to his office, he notices a glimpse of the white car again, down the street. Quickly getting into his car to give chase and finally get to see who this person is, Sam speeds off after it. Unfortunately, there is too much distance between them for Sam to catch up. It was as if they knew he was trying to follow. "For now," Sam thought to himself. "The white car shall remain a mystery I guess."

Chapter 9

Back at office, Sam calls out to Rachael as he enters. "Well, I'm back. Anyone miss me?" he says with a silly smile. "OH! Were you gone?" Rachael replies. "Man! Can you just feel the LOVE in this room?" Sam says laughingly as he walks to his desk shaking his head a little. As he sits at his desk, he notices he has a voice mail messages. As he access it to listen, he hears a familiar voice. The message is from Bill. "Hey Sam, Um ah... I thought about your offer and although I would like to take it, we have not yet tied up all our loose ends though. One of our shareholders has requested a meeting with me about something. I really need a little more time. Call me back as soon as you can so we can talk."
This is the second time now Sam has heard mention of a person that seems to have something over Bill or wants to talk turkey about the Buy out. Either way, Sam knows this is not a good sign and needs to act fast. Over the intercom he commands, "Rachael, get Bill on the phone right away Please." Shortly, Rachael informs him that Bill is on line two. Sam picks up the line and begins sternly, "Hello there, Bill. What's up with this stockholder of yours that seems to be holding things up? I'm NOT going any higher on this."

Bill then responds cautiously, "Well, Sam, it's like I said in my message to you earlier, this lady..." "LADY?" Sam interrupts loudly. "I mean this stockholder," Bill quickly changes "Has yet to meet with me with whatever it is they feel is so important. So, I really must acknowledge any concerns our associates may have regarding this matter. "Sam listens impatiently as Bill continues. "I have a meeting set up for first thing Monday to see what they have to say. This PERSON tells me they have an idea so I'm going to listen.

Let's extend your offer 'til Tuesday, O.K.?"

Sam thinks for a moment before uttering, "Bill, sounds like you're covering something up here. 10 a.m. Tuesday is as far as I'll go. Beyond that, you can just fall apart as far as I'm concerned. What time is your meeting on Monday? Maybe, I should be there... You know, in case there are any questions this "person" may have that I can help answer." Bill then told Sam that he had thought of that too but the other party wanted a closed door meeting with just him alone.

Sam was not happy with this at all, but he let it drop for now saying, "Suit yourself." Bill reassured once more, that he would call Sam as soon as the meeting was over and they could talk. Sam irritatingly acknowledges Bill's closing comments and abruptly ends the call. Returning to his voice mail, he listens to rest of his messages. There is nothing urgent, just the usual BS and questions. However, when Sam gets to his last message, he hears in an obviously altered voice, "Leave AMTRON alone, it's MINE! You don't understand the situation here."

Sam repeatedly listens to the message, trying to make out the voice, but his efforts proved to be unsuccessful. He calls Rachael into his office and questions her about the call.

Sam has her listen to the message and then asks what she makes of it. "This message came in at 1:45 this afternoon. Do you recall speaking with this caller?" Sam expresses tremendous concern in his voice as he asks.

"The only person that called around then was a man calling about a software idea he wanted to talk to you about." Rachael told Sam and then added. "But the voice from the message you just played, sounds more like a woman's." Sam looks at her with concern and tells her that if this person calls again to get a name and number before going into Voice mail. He does not want to get anymore strange threatening type calls. Rachael agrees and the then returns to her desk.

Sam kept thinking about Bills comment. Did Bill slip up when he said "lady" or was he playing some mind game, hoping the price would go up? One thing for sure, Sam has his mind made up that he is going to be in that meeting somehow. Sam clears his thoughts and starts to return his other calls. After then reviewing a few files on the present status of his own company, Sam reclines in his high back leather chair, staring out his window 21 stories up. Unwinding and starting to relax a bit, he begins to think about his weekend plans with Kathy. Rachael buzzes in, putting an end to Sam's little daydream. "Sir, are you going to be needing anything else today from me? It's 4 o'clock and I have a few things I would like to do on the way home before the bank closes"

There is no reply at all from Sam. Concerned, Rachael gets up and enters his office. "Is everything OK? Rachael asks. Sam turns to look at her and says "What? I'm sorry, I wasn't really listening." Rachael repeats her request and he tells her to go, he'll lock up when he leaves. Rachael smiles and says good night. When Rachael returns to her desk to shut down at her computer, the phone rings. Upon answering it, Rachael hears a voice that sounds a lot like the one in question.

Quickly she informs Sam before she transfers the call. Sam answers the phone as Rachael waits at her desk in case she is needed. Not at all because her curiosity is killing her. "Hello, What can I do for you?" Sam says to the caller. There is a momentary pause, then a click, soon Dial tone follows. Rachael enters the room. "So, what did they say?" she asks.

"Nothing, nothing at all. They just hung up." Sam tells her with a baffled look on his face.

Sam then adds, "First thing tomorrow I want you to get that phone guy out here and have Caller I.D. activated on your phone." "I'll give them a call first thing tomorrow. Are you going to be okay? Is there anything I can do for ya?" Rachael replies.

"No, you just go get your stuff done and I'll see you

in the morning." Sam assures her. Rachael gives him a little hug and goes on her way after leaving a note to herself about the Caller ID. Sam too, gets his things ready to leave. First however, he sits down and tries to call Kathy first. Adam answers the phone again, this time though, Sam asks for Kathy.

"Sorry about this morning," Adam said, recognizing the voice from this morning "But I didn't know she gave you a different name. Must be a girl thing" he added. Sam told Adam what Kathy said as to why she did that and everything was just fine. Sam then asked again for her. Adam explained that she just flew out the door but did say she would be right back.

"Please tell her I called and I'll try back again later then." Sam asked. "Sure thing! Talk to you later" Adam said and then hung up the phone. Sam then picked up his things and locked the office as he left. Getting to his car, he noticed a little note on his window just under the wiper blade. Setting down his briefcase, Sam picked up the note to read it. "Hello

Sam! Just me. Had a second so I thought I would leave ya little note about this weekend…YES!! Call me later at home I'll be there around 6 p.m.," it was signed Kathy. Sam puts the note in his pocket as he gets into his car to drive home. The note really made Sam smile, forgetting all about the strange calls he had gotten earlier. All the way home, Sam thought about the weekend and what all he had planed for the two of them.

Chapter 10

Pulling into his drive way he noticed the landscapers had not come out today. He parks and then looks around, wondering why they didn't show up. Upon entering the house, Shannon greets him, right away telling him about the yard and that they would be out first thing in the morning. Sam looks at her and then looks down a bit. "I wonder what ELSE is going to happen today?" Sam scoffs, as he puts down his stuff.
"Hard day at the office, Dear?" Shannon says mockingly. "Not bad, just really strange. So, what's for dinner?" Sam replies. His frame of mind now quickly changes as Shannon looks at him and just smiles with her head tilted just a bit. She always did know what to do to get Sam's mind off of work.

As Shannon proceeds to tell him what she plans on making for dinner, Sam just sits at the table with a sort of blank look upon his face. He stares out the window, Shannon notices and continues with the menu for tonight. "And then, for dessert, ME on a bear skin rug butt naked!"

That got Sam's attention, without turning his head or even blinking, he replied "Sounds good to me." Shannon did not expect an answer like that and remarked "Either you didn't hear a word I said or we need to talk! Now what's bugging ya?" Sam just looks at her and cannot hold back the smile any longer, saying "Just kidding. I have a lot on my mind is all. Got a couple of strange calls at work and it seems someone in a white car has taken a special interest in me. It showed up every where I went."

Shannon agreed that it sounded a bit odd and asked if Sam thought it had anything to do with the AMTRON deal. "Could be, but why now? What's different than last week?" Shannon sits down to listen as Sam continues. "They did tell me that there is some stockholder involved. Seems to me, it's messing up the whole deal. I don't know WHAT to think anymore." He looks to her for resolution to these dilemmas. Shannon thinks for a moment and then says, "Tell you what. Dinner won't be for about an hour yet". So, why don't you just go sit in the Hot Tub for a bit and try to relax." She gently rubs his arm as he rests it on the table.

"Yeah, that's sounds good. Think I'll do that" Sam replies as he then gets up from the table and walks out. Shannon starts to prepare dinner as Sam relaxes in the Hot Tub, letting his mind just wander and drift off. The warm rushing water and the sound it makes, lulls him to a gentle relaxing sleep. Thoughts now form images in his mind. The feel of the water brings him to a certain night, upon a certain boat. Reliving once more, the touch of his departed wife. Her arms, holding him gently. Sam smiles and continues with his dream.

Suddenly it all changes and he finds himself alone, along a shore line. In the distance is the silhouette of a woman, her arms out reached and running in his direction but not getting any closer. He walks toward her as if to be pushed along. The face never getting any clearer yet he does get closer. Her baggy flowing gown billows as if in a strong breeze. The water turns dark, becoming violent. As he reaches her, she holds out one hand in a motion that she wants him to stop.

Clouds roll in, covering the sunshine. There is not a sound as Sam stands still, looking at her, asking who she is. The reply was soft spoken. "You know who I am, and yet you don't know me at all" is all she said. Sam was close enough for the lady to touch his shoulder. An all too familiar feeling came over him. But before he could say another word, A voice seemed to come from nowhere. "Dinner will be ready in just a bit so you might want to get dried off and come on in." Sam opened his eyes slowly, ending the dream and seeing Shannon standing by him with one hand on his shoulder to wake him gently.

Sam stretches a bit and tells her he'll be right out. He walks up to his room and thinks about the dream while he getting dressed for dinner. As Sam Returns downstairs he hears Shannon, "So," Shannon starts "Do you feel any better now? Got things all under control?" "I feel much better now actually. I need to make a real quick call first, so just serve the dinner S L O W L Y, Okay?" Sam walks to the den and then calls Kathy. Kathy answers the phone this time. Sam is exhilarated to hear her voice and Kathy his.

"Hello there Darlin." Sam says softly. "I got your message" Kathy smiles on the other end saying "I was hoping you wouldn't mind me leaving it like that, but I was in a hurry to get to the store and pick up a few things for dinner tonight. Seems they kind of think I'm the maid around here." He hears her chuckle light heartedly as she tell him this and continue, "I don't mind though, they're letting me stay here all month and without charging me for anything, so, it's the least I can do."

Sam and Kathy talk for a few minutes, deciding on the Saturday afternoon pick-up time for their little weekend getaway. Soon, Kathy and Sam agree on the plans and hang up. Quickly and with a smile, Sam walks into the dinning room and sits. Shannon enters now and also sits at the table, asking Sam who he had to called so quickly. Sam just sort of looked at Shannon and with a little laugh said, "Well if you really must know, it was Kathy. We are planning on going out over the weekend. I was going to tell you about it."

Shannon sits up real straight, and with a little wink she replies, "Going to take the jet and go to the Casino over on the Main land?" Sam looked a little puzzled, asking how she guessed that. "Just a woman's intuition." Shannon answered. Sam sounded like a little kid at Christmas Time, going over the trip with Shannon. Its been a long time since he has showed this much interest in a lady ever since his wife past away a few years back. Shannon was torn between feeling good for Sam that he seems to be going back to his old self and at the same time feeling worried he might be headed for a fall.

"I'm sure she'll like it." Shannon says rather coolly. "So, what time should I be ready to go?" Shannon quizzes. "What?" Sam says as he stops eating and looks up, trying to see if she is joking or not. "Well, what am I supposed to do all day while you are off just flying around having a good time? You never take ME anywhere anymore." Shannon says with her little lip sticking out and using those puppy dog eyes to really get to Sam. Sam tries to say something but all that comes out is "Uh…Well I… uh… Shannon starts to laugh and mocks, "I I I I... uh.., Come on, you can do better than that! What's the matter, cat got your tongue? I'm just teasing with you. You two go and have good time. But I want to hear all the details when you get back"

Sam grins at her and says "Well, how about I just video tape it for you? Then, you can get the full effect?" Shannon smiles, her eyes grow wide and sparkle, "Hmmmm, Now your thinking!!!" Sam is left speechless for the firs time in his life. Seems Shannon is showing a side he is not familiar with. "Ooooo. Kkkkkk then!" Is all Sam says as he goes back to finishing dinner. Shannon laughs because she finally got him at his own humor and left him speechless.

When dinner was finished, Sam went to the living room to watch a little TV while letting supper settle. Shannon cleans up the kitchen and then decides to join him. As she sits next to him on the couch, she looks over and decides to let him off the hook, telling him she was only kidding about the Video thing. "Oh, it didn't throw me, I was just thinking of what the best angle would be for you!" Sam states.

They both laughed. Shannon then asked if he would like a drink while they watched a movie. Sam found this to be a good idea, perhaps giving just the right end to such a strange day. Shannon quickly gets up and makes a couple of drinks, Mudslides, Sam's favorite. Carrying a full pitcher and two glasses on a tray, Shannon walks over to set them down on the little coffee table. Sam's eyes got a little big, as he looked at the pitcher now before him. "Well!" he remarks, "Must a be long movie I guess." Shannon says nothing as she sits down beside him and pours. They both sit back now with their drinks in hand and relax as the movie begins.

After a few drinks, Sam and Shannon both are getting a bit happy and relaxed. Sam leans forward a bit and stretches his neck, closing his eyes a bit. Shannon looks over and says "Here, let me help you."

With that, she reaches over and rubs Sam's neck gently yet with a firm hand. As the rub penetrated deeply, Sam took a long drawn out breath of relaxing pleasure. After a minute or two, Shannon decides to slide a little closer. She leans across the couch, to reach his neck and shoulders better. "You could make a living at this," Sam remarks. Shannon perks up a little responding with, "Really, well, just leave some money on the table when I'm done." "What ever you want, just don't stop." Sam says back. After a few more minutes, a certain feeling seems to start coming over both of them.

The movie is now ending. Sam gently takes Shannon's hands from his shoulders and kisses them tenderly as he looks up into her eyes. Shannon heart seems to beat a little stronger as Sam gently but firmly holds her hands close together. Continuing to look her in the eye, Sam leans in for a subtle little kiss on cheek. Taking a deep breath, he says to her in a soft, almost distant sounding voice, "It's getting late Shan, I really must be getting to bed now. Good-night. I'll see you in the morning." Sam then pulls her up to her feet and gives her a warm tender hug before retiring for the evening.

Shannon stood there and simply said "Yeah, Good night!" Dazed for a few minutes, she then thinks to herself…. "O.K., what just happened here?" Although she was puzzled and a little confused, Shannon felt so much excitement. She continued to ponder. Sam has always made remarks to her and given hugs and little peck like kisses before, but never quite like this. It was always just friend's stuff. Shannon could tell something was going on here but was not sure exactly what to think of it.

After all, Sam is quite good looking and knows how to really treat a woman. The money thing of course is a plus, she also thought to herself with a little smile on her face. Shannon's thoughts continued until she started to quietly laugh at the absurdity in her runaway thoughts. Walking over, Shannon turns off the TV. Then returning the tray, pitcher and glasses to the kitchen, she rinses them out, turns off the lights and goes on her way to bed as well. Walking up the stairs, she hears Sam, humming to himself. Casually, Shannon looks over toward his room as she walks by.

Sam's light by his bed is on. Just curious, Shannon peeks in at the partially opened door to Sam's room. She notices he has just come from the shower and so he has nothing on at all as he walks toward his bed to get in and sleep. "Ooooooh Weeeee" she thinks to herself, quickly ducking back so she won't be seen. Sam was totally unaware of her spying eyes as he was climbing into bed. Shannon now stands up straight and Continues on to her own room after getting such a good eyeful.

As Shannon entered her room and closed the door behind her, she just smiled. Taking a few deep breaths she kept thinking "What a Kodak Moment!"

Chapter 11

For what seemed like hours, Sam laid there, his eyes closed but not asleep as he thought deeply about Kathy. Finally, he drifts into a dream of his weekend ahead. He can see her beautiful eyes and hear that angelic voice he finds so relaxing. Sam has only felt like this once before, over a lady named Robin.

Before long, sunlight comes through his window, all too early for Sam. Reluctantly, Sam wakens from his unconscious bliss. The alarm then blares with the arousing tone of the morning DJ on the radio. As Sam rises, he goes straight into his routine of preparing for a new work-day. After Sam is all dressed and ready, he goes downstairs, sits at the kitchen table says good morning to Shannon.

"So, sleep well?" Shannon asks, with the vision still in her head of what she saw the night before. "As a matter of fact," Sam exclaims, "I slept like a baby. Don't think I moved all night. How did you sleep?" Sam waited for a snappy answer, but all she said was, "Oh, I... slept well. Are you going to be working late today?" Sam told her he had only a few things to do and should be home at the usual 6 O'clock time frame. After a good breakfast, Sam grabs his briefcase and gives Shannon a little hug good-bye and then goes on to work.

Meanwhile, over at Kathy's, we find Kristy, Adams sister, Kathy's best friend, and Kathy having a rather interesting conversation. "I just can't believe you are actually going with him for the weekend." Kristy says with great concern. "Look, I really like this guy and I can see now why my sister married him. But I'm not going to tell him just yet who I am. Hell, I may never tell him and just disappear when all this is over. He sort of knows about me, though we've never met since I wasn't at their wedding. As far as I know, he's never even seen a picture of me. So how will he ever know unless SOMEBODY tips him off. I'm NOT out to hurt him. I just have plans for that Bill Butthead over at AMTRON." Kathy says, seeming a little nervous that Kristy may tell Sam who she is.

Kristy, taking a deep breath, remarks "Look, Kathy, I just don't like it when I see an innocent person possibly getting lead on. If you really like this guy then fine. Just don't use him like some pawn in your little game." "Don't worry" Kathy says "I know what I'm doing." Kathy looks over as Adam now enters the room. "Morning Ladies! What's up?" Adam says while slightly stretching.

Kristy pipes up first and says "I was telling Kathy to be careful. Do you know she is going off with Sam this weekend? I don't think it's a good idea at all." Adam looks at Kathy, seemingly a little puzzled. "I sure hope you have thought this over good," he tells Kathy. "Do you really know who this guy is? I mean, sure he's a nice guy and a pillar of the Island so to speak, but he's got a lot of clout and is NOT someone to screw with, if you know what I mean. Just be careful is all I got to say." Adam shakes his head a little as he walks over to get a cup of coffee.

"Some help YOU are, Brother!" Kristy says and then adds "Fine, you all just do whatever and leave me out of it." Kristy then takes a sip of her coffee and glares over at Adam. Adam see's this but ignores it and on walks over to sit down at the table. Kathy feels a little uncomfortable with the sudden tension going on in the room so she takes her coffee and returns to her bedroom. Sitting on her bed, Kathy thinks of her dear sister, Robin. A tear starts to form as she sorrowfully ponders. "WHY did it all have to happen this way? If only Robin had listened to me in the first place, perhaps it all would be different now." Kathy puts down her coffee now and quietly cries.

At the office, Sam goes through his daily planner to see what the day has in store for him. "Hmm, pretty light day." He thinks to himself. Rachael then enters the office to tell him the phone technician has come to setup the phone. Quickly, Sam gets up and walks out to tell him what is needed. Immediately the technician goes to begin his task. Approaching the phone room area, the technician notices someone rushing out, as if it were on fire. The figure scurries down the hall as the repairman enters the phone room. Looking around a bit, he finds no reason as to why that guy left in such a hurry. Since he noticed nothing out of the ordinary he went about his business and returns to Sam's office. He informs Rachael of the incident and remarked that since there is a recording device on one of lines then you should be able to match the voice recorded to the Caller ID number now too.

Rachael was puzzled over what he had told her since there was no recording device ordered to be installed that she knew of. Leaving her desk, Rachael went to see what he was talking about. The technician shows her what it was and how it's wired. He even showed her the little hook up for remote listening. Rachael quickly instructs him to disconnect it but make it look as if it had fallen off. That way, who ever put it here will be back to see why it is not working. With in seconds he has it unhooked and laying on the floor.

Rachael signs the man's work order and then goes to report this to Sam. "Sam?" She begins "...not sure how to tell you this but, a recorder was just found hooked up to our phone system. I had it turn off so that whoever did it will have to return to repair it." "GREAT!" Sam said throwing his hands in the air. "Mysterious cars, strange calls, Recorders! What's next? A man in a dark suit and glasses standing in the shadows?" Sam was totally infuriated now and for good reasons. "Keep an eye on that door and let me know if anyone goes in there, before you call security." he commanded.

Rachael acknowledged his request and went back to her desk. As the day continued, no one came by the watched room. It was very quiet in the office that day, mostly because Sam was not in a good mood at all. Kathy, meanwhile, is busy shopping for the weekend ahead. She decides on buying a nice negligee, just in case. She also thinks about all the things she needs to do before she leaves. Realizing that her mind really isn't much on shopping, she goes to the beach. Picking a nice large rock by the shore line she sits to unwind.

The memories of her sister, Robin, start to come to her, remembering the night Robin called her. It was the night before Robin died, when she had called. Robin had told Kathy about what she planned to do and why she was going to do it. No matter how much Kathy asked her not to though, Robin seemed possessed with the plan and would not listen at all. The words Robin said kept going over and over in Kathy's mind, as if it were happening all over again. Taking blame for what had happened. Suddenly, a large wave hits up against the rock, splashing Kathy in the face a little, snapping her out of her little trance. realizing that she has sat too long now, Kathy rose up to head home.

    Back at the office, Sam is on the phone when Rachael walks in to tell him she just saw someone quietly walking into the phone room down the hall. Quickly, Sam gets off the phone and tells her to call security right away. As Sam rushes to the room and enters, he is astonished to find one of his own workers inside. "John!" exclaims Sam. "What are you doing in here?" John, looking rather uneasy, asks what Sam is talking about. John didn't know Sam already knew about the recorder but figured out quickly what Sam was talking about by the way he kept looking at it.

    John starts to explain how he put a recorder on the line to record conversations between he and Bill. Sam grew quite angry at John and interrupted. "Just stop. You can't even look me in the face when you talk, how can I believe you? Now tell me what's going on here or you can just go pack up your office and leave." John was very serious. Shaking a little, John looked Sam in the face and answered, "O.K., O.K. I'll tell you" Taking a deep slow breath, John continues "I had a recorder hooked up to my line so I could record certain calls I was getting from some lunatic giving me subtle threats. I can even replay the recording from my office so I don't have to go in here to listen to it. I didn't want to tell you till I had something to go as to who it was."

    "O.K. Look," Sam says, "I can understand why you did this but why the lie in the beginning?" John had no answer so Sam adds "Take the rest of what's left of the day off and we'll talk more about this on Monday. Sam then turns and walks back to his office with astounding disbelief of all the events that have been going on the past week or so. He also finds it very odd that it all this started when Kathy showed up. "But that's ridiculous," Sam thought. What would SHE have to do with any of this?" Sam then decides to finish up a little early and leave.

He informs Rachael that he will see her in the morning on Monday and just lock up when she done. Rachael agrees and wishes him a good night. Sam did not listening to what Rachael said with his mind so preoccupied with other things. He just walks out the door and down to his car.

Chapter 12

Sam gets into his car and drives off to the hanger where his plane is. He parks and gets out slowly, his mind still a little uneasy from all the things he is trying to figure out. He enters the hanger and walks over to the maintenance crew, informing then to have his jet ready for flight on Saturday before 1 p.m. Sam then goes over the flight plan with the tower. After it is all settled and the times and route are on paper, Sam says good night and returns to his car to go home.

As Sam enters driveway, he sees the grounds crew busy finishing up the landscaping. Sam smiles, thinking to himself, Finally, Something is happening right. He walks into the house but does not see Shannon around. Sam then walks straight to the den and calls the hotel to reserve a room for the weekend, along with a car rental.

Shannon, hearing someone in the house, soon enters the den to see who is using the phone. She was all set to yell at one of the landscapers when to her surprise, she sees it's Sam. "Oh, it's you." She exclaimed "I couldn't tell who had come in, I'm sorry. You are a little sooner than you said, what's up?" Sam tells her he need to get away from work and get the arrangements for the weekend finished. Shannon listens intently as he then also tells her about John and the recorder deal.

"Sure was an interesting day for you then." Shannon responds, adding, "Do you want dinner early then since you are already home? Or would you mind me getting a few rays by the pool like I was going to before you got home?"

Sam thinks for a minute before noticing that Shannon already has her pool robe on. Rubbing the back of his neck a little he tells her, "Sure, go a head, knock yourself out. Just try not burn out there or come back in and burn supper either." Sam laughs and walks past Shannon to leave the room.

Shannon just looks at him, smiles and leaves the room to go off to the pool side. As Sam is up in his room, changing out of his work clothes, he hears the sound Shannon's radio coming from pool side. He walks out on his balcony to ask her to turn it down a bit and sees her laying there on the lounge chair in her little two piece swimsuit.

Sam stops and just stares, starting to think about how he used to see Robin lying out there when he would come home from work. She would be resting so peacefully, slow, even breathing, her skin shinny from the tanning oil.

Shannon suddenly had a feeling of being watched and opened one eye. Seeing Sam standing up above, looking down at her, Shannon was not sure what to think so she asked if there was something he wanted. Breaking Sam's train of thought, he stammered out "Umm, yeah, could you turn it down just a little please?" "Sure!" Shannon replied as she turned over to lower the volume and remained laying on her stomach.

Sam walked back into his room and then went downstairs to the den. Sitting back in his leather recliner, he started to fantazise about the weekend ahead. It seemed like only moments had pasted when he heard the opening and closing of the patio doors. Shannon was coming back in from her little rest and told Sam she would be getting dinner ready now.

The way Sam was laying back and looking at her, Shannon had a strange feeling come over her and she casually made sure he robe was closed. Sam just said OK about the dinner announcement as Shannon left the room to get dressed. She couldn't explain the feeling she had at first while she stood in front of Sam like that nor why she covered up because of it. "Why was it different now? Since he had seen her that way before many times" She asked herself as she entered the room to changed. Shannon finally just figured he must have been thinking about that Kathy lady again. However it didn't explain the covering up she did. Perhaps she was bit jealous and felt uneasy. It keep at her the whole time she was preparing dinner.

When dinner was ready, Shannon called Sam into the dinning room. As the two sat down to eat, Shannon asks "So, What do you think is going on lately with all the stuff you told me earlier?" Sam thought for a minute and then responds "Not sure really, but it seems to tie in with this whole Amtron thing." Sam then just shakes his head now in disbelief of all the events and continues to eat. With a concerned look, Shannon tells him to relax, that he will figure this all out in no time. Sam just plays it off and agrees with her, saying he's just not thinking straight, right now. All he can think of is this coming weekend.

"So, have any plans yourself?" Sam says to quickly change the subject. "No! Just gong to hang out around here and relax since I won't have YOU to be picking up after." Shannon shows a huge smile when she finishes her statement. "That's good" Sam says, again not really hearing what she had just said. With that, Sam gets up from the table and tells her he is turning in early tonight to get plenty of rest since the little trip starts tomorrow.

Shannon just says O.K. and Good Night as Sam retires upstairs to his room. Half way up the stairs though, he turns and sees Shannon watching him. "So, you've never seen me walk up the steps before? What are you thinking?" Sam says sort of puzzled. "Oh, Nothing. Just go to bed and get your rest. It's just that I've never known YOU to have to rest up for anything before. Gee, getting OLD????" Shannon replies, with a feisty sort of tone and raising one eyebrow. "Oh Goodnight" Sam says with a chuckle and then continues on up the stairs. Shannon watches a little T.V. and thinks about Sam and his situation before also going to bed.

After getting a good nights sleep, Sam wakes before Shannon and sneaks over to her room. Slowly looking in, he sees she is still in bed and sound asleep. Boldly, Sam walks in and maintaining a straight face, he says, "Dang! What's guy gotta do to get Breakfast around here? Hell, it's almost time for lunch. You going to get those OLD bones out of bed? Huh!? Call me old will ya. I'm already dressed and ready to go. But Noooo, I gotta wait for the Queen of Sheba here" Sam stands at the foot of Shannon's bed with arms folded, laughing.

Shannon quickly stirs under her covers but does not jump. Opening one eye, she simply replies "Oh give me a break! I've already gotten up once this morning and set up stuff for the trip, stacked it by the door, made up the pancake batter, set up the coffee maker and all while YOU got your beauty rest! Old Man!" Shannon then breaks out a big smile and looks right at him. Without warning, Shannon throws back the blanket with one swift movement. Sam quickly turns away.

"What's the matter" she asked "never seen a YOUNG woman get out of her bed... WITH her clothes on?" Laughing hard, she adds "What did you think?" "I was going to flash you? You ain't getting that lucky". The look on Sam's face tells it all. Shannon had got him good this time. As she gets up out of bed and walks past Sam, she stops just long enough to say, "Amateur!" then leaves the room. Sam follows her path, telling her that he will get her one day, he ain't giving up. Shannon continues to laugh as the two enter the kitchen. She reminds him that he can keep trying like always but you gotta get up pretty early to pull one off over her. Picking up the newspaper, Sam shakes his head as he thumbs through it.

On the first page he turns to there is a large article about Amtron, telling about how they are planning a comeback. "What the Hell?" exclaims Sam. "Have you read this? I was just talking to Bill yesterday and he mentioned nothing about THIS!" Sam starts to look like he's going to blow. "Now, Now" Shannon says "Don't worry about it, you know how things get blown out of content and taken all wrong. Maybe they are trying to raise the interest of the company before the auction"

Sam raises an eyebrow and looks at her. "So, I suppose YOU know something about it all too, Huh? Am I the ONLY one in the dark here?" He asks sarcastically and then adds, "Well, I'll tell you what. I am NOT going let this get to me. I need to get ready and make sure the plane is loaded and warmed up. I think this little trip will do me good to get away for a bit" Sam puts down the paper and begins to eat his breakfast. For the rest of breakfast, Sam rambles on about his trip and his proposed agenda.

Shannon however, can't help the feeling that this whole trip thing may be major mistake on Sam's part. After all, he just met this lady. What could he possibly really know about her? Shannon has always worried and fretted over Sam. Even when his wife was still alive, Shannon was right there to listen and help. Deep down, Shannon cared for Sam way more than just as a boss. She knew though that she could never let him know that. Shannon remembers how happy Sam was when his wife, Robin, was around. Then how devastated he was when the accident happened. She didn't want to him get hurt like that again.

Sam soon finishes eating, gets up from the table and heads to the door. Picking up his gear, Sam packs it all into his car. "Well, I'm off to the airport now. I'll see in you Sunday night Shan!" Shannon steps out real quick to say good-bye and to please be careful. Sam gives her a little squeeze and tells her he will. Shannon kept her head down and looked into the car. Pretending she was just making sure he didn't forget anything. In reality, Shannon was hiding the tear that was forming because she really didn't want Sam to go. Something just wasn't right about all this, it was just not settling well at all with Shannon.

Quickly composing herself, Shannon says, "Looks like you got it all in there. Now get going before you run out of time to have fun!" Even with the good cover, Sam senses just a hint of a jealously or something in her tone. "Gnaw!" He thinks to himself, dismissing the thought. With a smile, Sam gets in his car and waves good-bye to Shannon. She stands there waving back, watching him drive off. Softly without hardly moving her lips Shannon utters "I'll miss you." Shannon then re-enters the house and closes the door.

Chapter 13

Arriving at the hanger, Sam carries his stuff from the car to the plane. As he was putting in the items, he hears a car pulling up, just outside the hanger. Quietly Sam walks over and looks out to see who it is. Sam was hoping it would be Kathy even though it was just a little early yet. As he looks, he sees it is indeed Kathy. Before she can get out her car, Sam quickly ducks back and runs over to the plane. As Kathy enters the hanger, all she sees is a man standing by a plane, seemingly working on it. Sam's back was all she could see, she had no idea it was Sam.

As Kathy got real close, Sam kept his face hidden and with a muffled voice said to her, " Help ya with something lady?" "Well," Kathy started, "I'm looking for Mr. Katz. Have you seen him?" Kathy doesn't have a clue that she is already talking to him. "Yeppers!" came the reply, "Saw 'em jus a bit ago. Went on down to the office over yonder. Said a lady might be here soon and to tell her where he was. You be that lady?"

Kathy thought it a little rude for this guy not at least look at her when he spoke. She held her temper though and just said yes and Thank-you.

As Kathy started to walk away, she heard the guy at the plane yell over to her "Oh, Hey! Are you really as good of a Kisser as he says you are? I mean he went on and on about it like it was an Olympic Event or something. You really that good!? Wouldn't mind findin out myself ya know. But then he also went on about your..." Kathy quickly interrupts.

Frustrated and almost stuttering as she spoke, Kathy interjects with "Excuse me but I don't think that's any of your business. And I really don't think he would have told you that, true or not. I really should tell him how rude you are and see what you have to say then."

Kathy's arms were folded as she held them tight against her. It was all she could do not to hit the guy. Then after a second of silence the man told her, "Oh Yeah? Well look here Missy…" Sam now turns to face her, flashes her a smile and showing those big baby blues of his. Kathy's jaw about hit the floor when she saw it was Sam, trying to play a little trick on her. Kathy didn't know if she should smack him one or just scream. Kathy chose to do both and then said to Sam, "What? O.K. I see how you are going to be on this trip. Well, two can play this little game ya know" Kathy then starts laughing.

Sam starts to think he may have gone a little to far with this one. He steps close to her and apologizes while putting his arms around her, giving her a gentle hug. Kathy just stands there at first and then hugs back. Sam looks down at her, thinking he is out of trouble now with her. Kathy softly says "Oh, it ain't over yet!" Reaching up to give him a soft little kiss, she then asks him to help with her stuff to get it on the plane. Quickly, Sam goes out and gets everything she wanted to bring and loads it on the plane.

When he was done, Kathy asked if the Pilot was here yet. Sam replied "Yeppers! Captain Buck Rogers at your service Ma'm!" Kathy looked at him, with a not so surprised look on her face. "You Fly too???? Is there anything you can't do?" She then winks at Sam and grins. Sam just looked up as if to be thinking and answered back "Depends on… who I'm with" Then gave a little laugh like a Frenchman.

"I see this is going to be an interesting trip" Kathy remarks as she smiles, shaking her head ever so slightly. A few more minor things are taken care of to ensure a safe flight and soon, Sam and Kathy are in the plane off to the runway. Making his approach for final clearance, he looks over to Kathy and says with a huge smile, "Ready to go!"

Kathy just nods her head a bit saying "Oh Yeah!!! Lets get this sucka in the air!" then gently gives Sam's hand a little squeeze. Sam calls for take off. The reply comes back that all is clear on runway 4 and have a great flight. As the plane builds speed down the runway, Kathy's heart builds speed too. Faster and faster the speed picks up and the feeling of the ground below seems to fall away as the two take flight to a weekend they will never forget.

Once in the air and leveled off. Sam switches to Auto Pilot and turns to talk to Kathy. He tells her about the things he has set up and hopes she will really enjoy it all. Kathy assures Sam that things will be just fine. After a few minutes up in the air, Kathy gets up to go to the back of the plane and check out the lounge area. He also told her to go ahead and fix herself a drink if she would like, or even take a little nap since the trip will be a few hours.

There was no way Kathy was going to be able to do any sleeping on this trip, being so keyed up and all. She went back and got a large glass of Tea, then returned to sit with Sam. She start talking and looking around and asking question after question to Sam about the plane and that she has never been to Vegas before and so on. Kathy didn't slow down from talking for even a minute. Sam could hardly get a word in edgewise let a lone actually give a full answer to even one of her questions.

Kathy seemed like a child at Christmas time. Sam really loved how much she seemed to be enjoying herself so far and didn't mind at all the constant talk all the way to their destination. Before either of them realized, they were approaching the Vegas air strip. "Umm, Darlin? I hate to interrupt but would you go back and see that everything is secured back there? We are going to be making our landing soon and I would hate for something to come flying up here in the middle of it."

Kathy agreed with a smile and went back to check on things. Sam cannot remember when he's felt this happy in such a long time. Kathy of course, kept talking even while being in the back of the plane.

Chapter 14

Soon, they landed at the airport. Kathy can hardly sit still as she can't wait to see and do all the things Sam has talked about. As they come to a stop, a luggage handler comes out to get their stuff and bring it to their hotel. Kathy slowly gets off the plane, takes a deep breath and then looks at Sam. Sam smiles, telling her "Well, here we are! Lets get the car I have reserved." They both walk off to the Rental dept. and soon they are on their way. The Hotel was not far at all, so in just a few moments they were walking into their suite. It was a huge two bedroom set up with all the luxuries. As Kathy looked around, seemingly impressed, their luggage arrived. The carrier asked where they would like their bags placed. Sam told him and so in no time at all the luggage carrier placed each of their bags in their room.

Kathy went on in to her room to get ready for a night on the town. Sam sat at the little table that was setting by the balcony. Looking out over the city, he realized that he had forgotten how beautiful it all was. Sam had not been here since his wife passed away 4 years ago. Now he was here once more, with a lady that makes him feel alive again. After a little bit, Kathy comes out of her room saying "Ready or not, here I come!" Sam was left speechless, he couldn't believe how beautiful Kathy looked standing there in front of him.

At first, Kathy thought something was wrong since Sam had no comment. As she walked close though, she could see by the look in his eye that Sam was very happy. Without a word, Sam reached forward and gave her a hug. He then whispered in her ear about how beautiful she looked and how honored he was to be with her. Kathy smiled, and sort of blushed just a little with downcast eyes. Then, she reached up, flung her arms tightly around his neck. She kissed him so hard, he thought his teeth would fall out. "Now, it's your turn to go change?" she uttered almost seductively.

As Sam went in to change, Kathy now sat by the table and kept an eye at Sam's door to make sure he was not going to be coming right back out. When she felt she had some time, she took out her Cell phone. Quietly she dialed Kristy to let her know they made it safely. Once again Kristy voiced her disapproval of the whole thing, but stopped at that point. Kristy didn't want to start an argument right now so she kept most of her thoughts to herself. Kathy assured her things were going to be fine, she could handle what ever comes up. Sam finished getting ready a little sooner than Kathy had expected, so as the door open and Sam started to walk out, she quickly said good-bye to Kristy and hung up.

Sam asked who she was talking to and she told him she just called Kristy to let her know they made it OK. Then, she eyed Sam up one side and down the other. Giving a grand smile of approval she took his arm and they headed out. Once they got to the lobby, it was not long at all before the Valet brought up the car. Sam had rented a beautiful, sleek, black Corvette with white interior. The valet holds the door open for Kathy as she glides into her seat.

Sam eyes the Shape of her long legs and slender waist. "This is going to be a night to remember." Sam happily thought to himself. Kathy noticed Sam was watching her get in and decided to make it a bit seductive for him. Sitting in side ways, Kathy slowly swung one leg in and then the other. Sam tried to hide the enormous smile that he had and almost asked her to get out and do it again. After Kathy was settled, Sam went around to the other side to get in. With Kathy sitting by his side, looking so elegant, Sam felt he was on top of the world. With pride, Sam dropped the car in gear and sped off.

Soon, they arrive to their destination. Sam parks the car out front and the two notice that the sun is now setting. It casts an ominous glow upon the casino's alluring structure. Before getting out of the car, Sam looks over and at the wonderful smile on Kathy's face. Kathy shouts with glee,

"Let's break the bank!" Sam quickly steps out of the Corvette in his three-piece, black, pinstripe suit, custom fitted, with a tailored white shirt and a Sinsario red tie. He walks around to Kathy's side, opens the door and extends his hand to help her out.

As the two walk up to the entrance, Kathy is holding Sam's arm and walking with a smile. Heads turn as they walk by, noticing the lovely Kathy, dressed in a "V" cut, velvet, forest green, floor length formal gown. Her lengthy legs exposed by the equally lengthy side slit, showing off her curvaceous thighs, her sensually sculpted calves and even the elegantly glimmering bracelet that was around her dainty ankle.

Before entering the casino, they both stop, gaze up at the sky and make a wish on the first star they see. They both noticed the look in each other's eyes as they wished for a time to end all times. Arm in arm, they now enter. Everything seems so grand as they look around. Standing for a second, their ears fill with the sounds of the Slot machines, dealer calls, hoards of people, musical bands. Their eyes dance as they see lights flashing all over.

"It is ever so spectacular" Kathy remarks. As the two continue to look around, they find that they are a little indecisive on what to do first. A surge of excitement comes over them as they make their way through the room. Sam keeps hold of Kathy's arm and leads her to a set of large, wooden double doors near the rear of the Casino. "This evening is to start with a Dinner Show, I've decided," Sam tells her.

The room is dimly lit as they enter. A single light shown upon the stage in make ready for the Entertainment. The Host greets them quickly and seats them. Soon, the Maitre D comes over and Sam asks to see a wine list, Kathy interrupts Sam by saying, "Would you mind if we skipped the wine? I would really like a Banana Daiquiri." "Sure" Sam says "I'll have a screwdriver then, please" he orders to the Maitre D "Very well, Sir," the Maitre D says, then walks off to get of their order set up.

Noticing the little card on the table, Sam remarks, "Tonight is apparently being called, Magician's night with some comical twists." "Sounds interesting!" Kathy adds. A waiter then shows up at the table with their drinks. "Here you go sir and lady." "May I recommend the Steak and Lobster for Two?" It's the House Special tonight"

Sam looks at Kathy to see what her thoughts are on the suggestion by the waiter. Kathy loves a good steak so she tells him that will be fine with her. Sam instructs the waiter that they will both have tonight's special. Asking all the questions as to how the steaks should be cooked and what side dishes they want, the waiter collects the menus and heads off to place the order with the chief.

Upon finishing their first drink, they order another. Not too long after the second drink arrives, the server brings out their meal. Before the server was finished placing the plates on the table, the show began to start. The lights were turned the rest of the way down so that only the stage is lit up. The MC comes out and announces the Entertainer for tonight and hopes everyone enjoys the show. As the Magician walks out to center stage, a spot light follows. Sam watches very closely at the Magician's every move, in hopes to catch the secret of how it's done.

The show is really quite grand, as the dinner is beyond compare. Both Sam and Kathy are quite delighted. Sam looks at Kathy's profile as she watches the show. As Kathy laughs, a strange sort of Dejavo comes over Sam. It was as if he was looking at Robin, but why did he feel that way, Sam thought to himself.

Kathy turned, noticing Sam staring at her. "What's the matter? Show getting boring for you? Have it all figured out?" She says. Sam suddenly snapped to and responded "No. Just watching you smiling and how much you seem to be enjoying yourself. It does my heart good to hear a woman laugh. Unless of course it's when she is looking at me naked" He says with a little laugh and raises his eyebrow suggestively.

"Come on, the show is over now. Let's go place some bets. Are you feeling lucky?" he adds. "Hmm, I think YOU are!" Kathy adds in response to his little naked humor and laughs. They left the dinning room and went straight over to the cashier. Sam takes out his check book to buy some chips. When the cashier sees the name, she remarks "Samuel Katz? I thought you looked familiar. I saw your picture in the paper the other day. Also, haven't I seen you in here before?" Sam thinks for a moment and sees Kathy looking at him with a wondering look in her eye. As if to say, "So, you bring ALL your dates here?"

"Well," Sam begins "I was here before but that was a long time ago. I came here with my wife before she died. I have tried so hard to not think about the past, that I didn't even realize…." The cashier interrupts quickly "I'm sorry, I didn't mean to upset you or anything. You both just looked so familiar is all. I remember faces pretty well"

"That's O.K" Sam says "You didn't know. Now, where's our chips?" Sam looks at Kathy and she asks him, "You sure you want to stay? I mean with the memories and all." Sam just half smiles and tells her they are there to brake the Bank and nothing is going to stop that. Kathy takes his arm and smiles as they look over the room to pick their game of chance. Slot machines, card tables, dice, roulette, what ever shall they do first? They both thought hard about it.

They simply looked at each other with confusion and an inner excitement. Kathy finally remarks that she wants to try it all and so does he. Pulling out a coin, Sam tells her to call it, heads, cards; tails, dice. The coin goes up, then down it comes as Kathy blurts, "Heads". The coin lands heads up. "So Blackjack it is then" Sam says as they make their way to the dealer. Sitting on the stool, Kathy and Sam are dealt into the game. So now the betting begins. Starting with five and winning 10, they double down and do it again. After a few hands, their winnings really start to grow as does the excitement.

Kathy can hardly contain herself as a few more hands are dealt and a few more wins are made. Kathy starts to look around a little as the hands are being dealt, to line up the next betting adventure. "Roulette!" Kathy blurts out "Now there's a game." Sam agrees. Finishing the last hand, they walk on over to try their luck at the wheel. With a one big spin, all bets are in. Kathy squeezes Sam's arm a bit in anticipation as they watch it go around and around, ever so slowly coming to a stop.

Kathy just can't take the suspense so she closes her eyes. "31 Black!" is the number she hears called out. She bet 17 red so she lets out a little moan as she pulls strongly on Sam's arm. Going to the next table then, to try their luck, they break even. Sam could see Kathy is not having as much fun as before so he brings her attention to the slots. As the two walked on over, Kathy eyes up a large one, sitting in the middle of the room. It's a Ten dollar slot with a huge payoff, if you are lucky enough to hit it right.

She leans into Sam as they walk, getting him to go in the direction of the one she cannot take her eyes off of. Sam hands Kathy some coins as she puts them in one by one. With a little moment of silence, Kathy gives it a mighty pull. One bar clicks in, two bars click into place, now Kathy really smiling as she peeks out between her fingers that are across her face. She watches as the last spot drops into place. "An Orange!?" Kathy exclaims "What the Hell….. O.K. One more try". The excitement begins all over again.

Triple Bar, Triple Bar,… the last click is heard as she sees the third Triple Bar drop in place. All of a sudden, lights are flashing, bells are ringing, voices all around are cheering for them. Kathy had hit the big jackpot, One Million Dollars. She didn't know what to say as she stood there staring at the large windows of the slot machine. After a few minutes, she regains her speech and whispers something in Sam's ear.

A look of surprise comes over him as he listened to her idea. Sam agrees and with a huge smile he signals for the Pit Boss to come on over. After Sam tells the man what they wish do, Kathy and Sam go about doing a little more gambling, before returning to their Hotel. After an hour or two more goes by, Sam and Kathy agree it is time to cash out their remaining chips and leave. Sam has a Valet brings the car around while they are doing this.

Chapter 15

Hardly a word is said during the drive back. Excited glances are all that's done. Though Sam and Kathy were quite tired, they are not sleepy at all. As Sam parks the car at their Hotel, Kathy gets out before he even turns off the engine this time. "Gee, a little excited, are we?" Sam says with a smile. Kathy says not a word, as she takes his hand leading him quickly into the Hotel and to the elevator.

She grows impatient as the elevator seems to take forever to open. Rushing in before Sam, Kathy turns and says "Come on, unless you plan on taking the stairs!" Sam gets in, a long embrace takes place as the Elevator works it's way up to their floor. As it comes to a stop and the door reopens, Kathy pauses for a moment making the embrace last a little longer before walking down the hallway to their room. Sam unlocks and opens their suite slowly. The smell of money is all around. There, as instructed, in the middle of the room, was the biggest pile of money Kathy had ever seen at one time. Her eyes grew large, like a little kid at Christmas.

Sam can see the excitement in Kathy's eyes, so with one quick motion he sweeps her off her feet and carries her to the pile of money. Gently, Sam then rests her down into it. The bills move around like a pile of leaves in the fall, almost completely engulfing Kathy. With a big smile on her face, Kathy looks up at Sam, saying "Care to join me?". Giving Sam a subtle little wink, he now kneels down in front of her.

As Sam gets real close, she grabs each side of his face, tenderly gives him a kiss to end all kisses. The sound of money reselling beneath, added to the excitement of the kiss. Sam pulls back after a moment, looks deep into her eyes seeing the sparkle of starlight. The physical tension was now rising inside both of them. Hearts were pounding fast, breathing was slow and strong. Between the excitement of the evening, the drinks, the laughter, and being in the arms of a beautiful woman, Sam's feelings that he had locked away for so many years and had thought were gone, were now starting to emerge once more.

Kathy strokes the side of Sam's face, feeling his skin against the back of her fingers. He places a hand upon hers and glides it to his lips, tenderly kissing her fingertips. Without a word, Sam gets up to turn on some soft music and turn down the lights just a little bit. Kathy watches as he walks back, totally caught up n the moment. After loosening his tie and kicking off his shoes, Sam sits back down by Kathy and once more takes her hands.

Sam slides in even closer, looking deeply into Kathy's eyes. His loneliness that has built over the years seems to melt away with every passing second. Placing his hands along both sides of Kathy's face, Sam kisses her tenderly at first, then harder. His pressed so hard that Kathy had to pull back and take a breath. She was bit taken by the forcefulness of Sam, he had always been so gentle up to now and didn't know what to make of it. Kathy was not upset though, as she enjoyed it immensely. Kathy smiled at Sam and she regained her breath she wanted more.

Slowly the kisses became hotter and moved lower down her neck. With every passing moment the passion and want inside Kathy grew. She had never experienced such a deep and strong passion s Sam was giving. Soon, Kathy's hands were traveling across Sam's body, caressing and rubbing. Kathy took a quick, deep breath, sitting up straight as Sam moved around behind, to unzip the back of her dress. Slowly, Sam kissed his way down as dress opened. Kathy turned to face him. Sam held on to the dress, removing it, exposing Kathy's fine tan body. Kathy then reached out to unbutton Sam's shirt and remove his tie. In a few moments, the two laid there, surrounded in the pile of money, almost naked. Soft whispers and subtle little moans were all that could be heard amongst the soft music and sound of rustling money. Each, now let loose of all inhabitations and hesitations. Allowing the delight and ecstasy ahead completely take over.

Sam and Kathy were breathing hard as the last bit of clothing came off. Sam continued to caress and nibble on Kathy, enjoying every moment of Kathy's touch. Soon, feeling of Sam, deep inside, went beyond what Kathy had ever felt before. Thoughts started to flood and build as Sam and Kathy grew close to completion. With in seconds after climax, other visions suddenly entered Sam's mind. Sam rolled to his side and looked at Kathy as he held her close in his arms. Was it the drinks, the atmosphere or the fact that this is where he and Robin used to get away to a lot? Sam could not quite shack her image from his mind. Kathy just looked at him, not knowing what was actually going through his mind. She only saw a look of content and felt safe and warm as he held her close.

As the music played in the background, Sam shook the feeling and images from his mind. One more passionate kiss was shared between Sam and Kathy as they laid there now in each other arms. Their hearts still beating hard against their chest, now started to slow down. As Kathy drifted off into a gentle slumber, Sam kissed the top of her head and whispered, Good Night Darlin. Swiftly, Sam picked her up in his arms and placed her in bed. As he covered her, he saw the smile on her face as continued to sleep. Kissing her on the head, Sam then went around to the other side of the bed and slipped in under the sheets. Almost before his head hit the pillow, Sam was sound a sleep.

As morning came, The sun's first rays hit Sam in the face. Placing one hand in front of his eyes, he slowly opened them, turning his head, he saw Kathy, laying along side him, curled up like a child. She looked so innocent and carefree, still with a slight smile from the enjoyment of last night. Sam tried to get up without waking her, but as he moved, Kathy's eyes opened. Her smile grew even larger as she gazed at Sam, now sitting up beside her. She reached toward him to placed her arms around his waist. Hugging him strongly, she said Good Morning. Softly, Sam returned the good morning and then added that they needed to get up and dressed and then pack up all this stuff all over the floor.

"Just a few more minutes." Kathy uttered with her eyes now closed again. Sam said OK but got up any way. He was dressed and ready after a nice refreshing shower. He entered back into the bedroom and saw that Kathy had already gotten up. Looking at the pile still on the floor, he started to recall the feeling and emotion that Kathy had given, along with the tender caressing. Sam looked around and found she was sitting by the balcony with a cup of coffee she had ordered from room service. There was second cup too, for Sam.

"Oh good, Coffee!" Sam exclaimed as he picked it up for a sip. Kathy asked if he slept well and Sam assured her that he slept like a baby. He also asked her jokingly if she was going to be leaving the Hotel and flying back in just her robe. Kathy kept a straight face and asked if that would be a problem. Not being able to hold back the smile though, Kathy gave it away that she was joking around with him. She got up with the coffee and walked off to her room to get dressed. When she walked by the pile of money on the floor, Kathy stopped and sighed slightly, remembering the wonderful night. Bending down, she then pulled dress out that was buried in the pile, along with her shoes

Sam watched as she moved about the room, collecting her things from last night. A sudden chill came over him. Sam just took another sip of coffee and stared out the window. After a few moments, Kathy came out and walked over to sit by Sam at the table. She could tell something was on his mind but was not sure if she should ask. Sam did not say much as he sat there, drinking his coffee. Finally Kathy did ask what was on his mind. "Are you thinking what happened last night?" she uttered.

Sam did not answer right away. Slowly, Sam put down his cup first before saying, "Last night was fantastic Darlin. I can't remember when I have felt so alive. It's been years. It was like you and I have been together for a long time. It all just felt so perfect. I guess that's what's bothering me a little. I hardly know you and you hardly know me yet I feel as though we've been around together for a years. I feel so comfortable when I'm around you. There's just something so familiar about you." Kathy smiled at his answer and said she very enjoyed last night too.

Kathy was now starting to feel a little guilt as to the truth of who she was and the fact that she is really falling for Sam big time. "None of this was supposed to happen," Kathy said to herself, as she continued to smile at Sam. All these thoughts and more, flashed through Kathy's head with in an instant. Sam broke her train of thought by asking if she would like some breakfast. Almost with a start, Kathy looked over at Sam and replied that breakfast sounded wonderful right now. She was quite relived that Sam had changed the subject before she said something that she shouldn't right now.

Soon, they departed downstairs to the car. Kathy, not knowing what to say right now with all the things going over in her mind, blurted out, "Half that money you know is really yours. You gave me the coin to use so we really should split it." Sam just laughed a little at Kathy's reasoning, turning down the offer and for her to please take it all.

Kathy thought to herself for a moment, that if she had a Million, then she would perhaps not have to deal with her silent partner in going after Bill. The more she thought the more uneasy she became, Kathy wanted Bill to pay for what he had done to her sister Robin, in a big way. After breakfast, Kathy and Sam decided to spend time in city before they flew back. A few hours were spent going in and out of every little shop they could find, exploring the streets and avenues. Neither of them could recall a time when they have had more fun.

Kathy was starting to get a bit tired, as was Sam, so they stopped at a little outdoor café restaurant to have a nice lunch. After they order and were waiting for the food, Sam asked Kathy what type of plans she had for the up coming week.

"Oh, just, relaxing. Nothing really important, why?" she asked in return. "Well, except for Mon. and Tue I'm pretty open, so I thought we could get together some more." "Monday?" Kathy interrupts "What's happening on Monday?" "Just some company business, I'm doing some….. I guess you could call, undercover work" Kathy starts to get a bit uneasy, trying not to let Sam notice.

Trying to find out more with out seeming obvious, Kathy remarked jokingly "Undercover Huh? You have someone else already waiting for you back at the Island? Hmm?" Sam sees her little smile, answering "Never know. I mean, you know how talented I am" He gives a wink and then starts to chuckle. "Really, as you know, I'm trying to buy out this company and I found out there's this secret meeting to take place on Monday afternoon. I need to, and will, find a way to either be there or at least find out who it's with."

Sam notices while he is talking, how Kathy seems to be becoming a bit uneasy. He stops what he is saying to ask, "What's wrong, You seem tense all of a sudden" Looking for the right thing to say, Kathy quickly replies "I just don't want you getting arrested or disappearing on me. I know how these corporate things work. I read the papers, people just one day become a memory. Let's forget about this and just continue our day. Or at least what's left of it." Kathy now hopes that she has changed Sam's mode of thinking. However all Sam did was file what she said in the back of his mind for now. Sam's curiosity of Kathy's interest in what's going on is more than just a concern for him and he knows that.

Kathy then adds, to change the subject, "This day sure has been a delight. I'm so glad we finally met" With out realizing what she had just actually said. Sam remarks with confusion "Finally Met? What do you mean by that?" "Oops!" Kathy thinks to herself just before saying, "What I mean is... You know, Um, when we met... You, met a lady named Dee, not the one sitting here by you now. I was just messing with you is all. Sorry about that." Sam Forces out a convincing little laugh, to cover the now strange feeling deep inside. "O.K., I see what you mean. We need to return to our room though and get packing." It takes about 30 minutes to get back to their hotel. Not much was said on the rest of the ride back. Each wanted to ask the other a million questions but did not want to perhaps end this trip on a sour note.

Sam is done packing before Kathy, so as he waits for her to finish, he calls for a bellboy to come up and get their things, figuring she should be done by the time the person gets up there. One down by the car, Sam stops and looks at Kathy standing there, just inside the shade of the building. The wind sort of blowing gently through her hair, Sam was a gain taken by what he saw. It was like something you would see in a movie, or read about in a romance novel.

◆

Kathy slowly walks on over as she sees Sam staring to the car door for her to get in. As Kathy starts to get in, she hesitates, stands back up and gives Sam a rather strong, firm hug. Then looks into his eyes, telling him "Thank-you for the most wonderful time I've ever had" Sam detected a tear starting to form in Katy's eye. With understanding sort of smile, He tells her "Well, we could stay one more night and get an early start in the morning to go back. I Don't need to really be anywhere till the afternoon," Sam holds her gently in his arms as awaits an answer.

"I wish I could" she replied "But I made promises for tomorrow. I'm supposed to get with my friend, I don't want to let her down, she has planed this ever since I first mentioned coming out to the Island. There will be other times though I hope, and we'll make it longer then, O.K.?" Kathy asks with a total hope for a yes answer. Sam taking a deep breath, pushes back a bit to look at her. His heart, obviously feeling a bit hurt from her answer, replies "O.K., we can... do this again sometime, I understand about friends and promises" Kathy is relieved and tells him thank-you for understanding. The two embrace for a moment, giving each other a kiss to end all kisses. Kathy them lets go and slowly gets into the car as Sam stands there, holding the door and looking at her. Sam goes around after closing her door, to get in and start the drive back to the airport. The plane is already waiting on them.

Chapter 16

Once at the hanger, everything is quickly loaded as Sam makes the final check up in the Cockpit. Kathy sits by his side, watching. After a few minutes, Sam gets clearance to take off. As he is taxing down the runway, Kathy gives him a little kiss on the cheek, again telling him thank-you for such a wonderful weekend. A few moments after take off, Sam levels off, turns to Kathy and tells her with a smile, that if she's tired it would be OK to go in the back and take a little nap.

Kathy was not in the napping mood though, she wanted to stay up front, with Sam. The sun seemed to highlight the few clouds that were there, giving the sky a very relaxing atmosphere. They talked for a bit, one thing leading to another, both staying away form anything having to do with AMTRON. Before long, the relaxing motion of the plane started to take its toll on Kathy. Unbuckling her seatbelt, she told Sam that was going to take him up on his offer of lying down for a bit. She gave him a little kiss and then went back to middle of the plane, where all the comforts of home were set up.

Lying down on the couch, she started to think. An idea came across Kathy's mind so she sat up, looking to see if Sam could see her form his seat up front. When she was sure he could not see her, Kathy took out her cell phone to make a quick little call. "Hello?, its me, Kathy. We're on our way back and things went just great. What's that? No, we didn't really talk about business stuff at all,... Really. I mean, he started to but I changed the subject. I did find out though that I need to be careful on Mon. at the meeting. I Know, I know, I'll handle it. I gotta go now before he hears me.... YES I'll be careful, Bye!" Kathy hung up, then took one more look to see if Sam was trying to look back. In order to convince herself that he could not hear her, she spoke in a voice that was the same level as the one used on the phone. "Sam? I'm butt naked and want you bad!" When she heard no reply, she relaxed in the feeling that he indeed did not hear her conversation on the phone. Kathy laid there a little longer, starting to rest, but could not get too comfortable due to the thoughts that kept playing over and over in her mind. She thought of all the things they had done through the weekend and wondered if Sam would have been the same towards her if he really knew who she was. The more she thought about it, the more she realized she may never be able to tell Sam the truth.

After a few more minutes of uneasy rest, Kathy returned to her seat next to Sam. Sam was not paying much attention though as he was looking down at the gauges when Kathy came up to sit. She sat for minute before asking, "How long have you been flying?" "Oh, about 45 minutes now." Sam laughed after saying that and then added "O.K., I've logged a lot of hours up here. I've flown through about every type of weather there is, in all kinds of situations. You're not getting nervous on me now are you?" Kathy simply replied "No, not nervous, just curious is all.

Sam was still concentrating on his instrument panel when she asked another question. "So, what is that you are looking at any way?" Upon asking this question, Sam looked up at her to explain,

Sam's eyes suddenly grew quite large as he looked over at Kathy sitting there. She was so beautiful, So,,,,,,, Naked!" Sam almost stuttered as he managed to say "Umm... ddid you... forget ssomething back ttthere?" "No, why?" she replied "You said you've been there done that in this plane" Kathy said with a smile, looking right into Sam's eyes. "Well, yeah. I mean sure, but I wasn't talking about having a Naked Co-pilot! I'm going to have to take you places more often" Sam says with a big smile.

Kathy continues to look over at him, now with a little devilish grin upon her face. Subtly, Kathy reaches toward Sam, saying "Lets see now, this is the Joy stick, right?" Sam took a quick breath, then saw she actually was pointing to the plane's joy stick control. "Well, yeah, that's one of the joy sticks up here" Sam replies with a smile, hoping she will continue her quest for knowledge, so to speak. "Hmm, I thought so" was all Kathy said as she sat back fully into her seat. The seat reclined back just a bit, giving Sam full view of her sitting there. Kathy was enjoying the Hell out teasing him like this, watching him try to maintain control and pay attention to what he was doing.

They bantered back and forth for a bit before Sam thought Kathy looked like she was going to make her move. Sam, took the first move now and placed his hand on her leg. Kathy leaned toward him, she reached down and seductively took hold of Sam' hand that laid upon her leg. Slowly, Kathy made it glide across her skin. Sam grew quite excited as she maneuvered his hand slowly but swiftly up her body, across her chest, then back down to the other leg, without hesitation. He heard Kathy then say, in a low whisper, "Now, don't you need to be thinking about flying this thing? I'll just sit here and relax, while you fly."

Kathy places his hand back on the controls, leans back in her seat, takes a slow deep breath while stretching with her hands above her head "Now just pay attention to flying. Don't mind little old me sitting here. NAKED!" she says. Sam watches as she tilts her head back a bit and closes her eyes. Soon, Kathy has drifted off. After about ten or fifteen minutes, Sam calls her name softly, to make sure she is sound asleep. Next, he picks up the microphone to make an announcement, loudly so as to waken Kathy.

"Attention passengers! This is your Captain speaking. We are making our approach to our destination and will be touching down in about two minutes. Please, remember to secure all loose objects and wave at the tower as we land. Thank-you for flying Delta Nude Airlines!" With that, Kathy woke with a start! Trying the best she could to cover herself, she made a "B" line to the back of the plane. As Kathy to the back of the plane, she sort of stumbled, still being half asleep. Grabbing up her clothes frantically, she got dresses.

Sam could hear her yelling from where she was while dressing herself. "Funny, Very Funny….. I sat up there for YOU to see, not the whole damn Island. I mean really now, giving a two minute warning like that, what were you thinking….."

Sam could tell Kathy was getting bit ticked off over his little prank. Quickly, he got on the P.A., cutting right into what she was saying. "2

Minutes? Gee, I'm sorry….. I meant 2 HOURS!" Kathy stood there for a minute, slightly fuming. Without saying a word, she came back up front, fully dressed this time. She sat in the Co-Pilot's seat looked out the window, her arms folded in front of her. Sam could feel the tension and stopped laughing. Realizing he may have gone too far this time with his humor, he started to apologize.

Kathy looked over and piped up, "You little shit!" as she smacks him on the arm lightly. "You know, I WAS going to check out that OTHER joy stick you were talking about but NOPE, You blew it". "I blew it?" Sam says "But you just said You were going to do that….Oh wait, did you mean something else?" Sam's attempt at making light of the situation and getting her to laugh was not being received very well.

"WHAAATTT???" Kathy said "You really need to just fly the plane. You almost gave me a heart attack." After a moment of silence, Kathy started to smile. She realized, the more she thought of it, it was a little funny. She did like the way squirmed though, thinking he was really in hot water with her now. When Sam saw the smile, he too smiled back. Soon they were both laughing out loud about it. The rest of the trip home was back to being a pleasant one, as they talked and bantered all the way. Soon, Kathy could see the Island coming into view. "Sure does look pretty from up here doesn't it?" she remarked. "Yep, that's why I put my business here" Sam told her "Better buckle up though, we're heading in". Kathy was safely in her seat, as Sam made his approach to land.

As they were landing, Sam and Kathy were both wishing this weekend wasn't over yet. So as the plane came to a stop, they looked at each other. "Made it!" Sam said with grin." "In more ways than one!" Kathy thought to herself. As they left the plane, Sam asked one of crew at the hanger to please unload Kathy's stuff first and place it in her car for her. While this was being done, Sam invited Kathy into the office and then closed the door.

Sam held Kathy close, as he told her once more how wonderful she had the trip be. Kathy looked up at him saying "The pleasure was all mine really. I didn't know there were still such nice guys like you left. It's no wonder you… were married before". Sam smile as he looked into her eyes deeply. Slowly, he pulled her close, whispering in her ear "I wish this day would never end" then proceeded to give her a kiss that about knocked her shoes right off.

Kathy, now a little weak in the knees and sort of speechless, managed to say, "Well, I…. Need to be… going now" Sam Smiled and said nothing as he walked her to her car and helped her get in. He stood there and watched as Kathy fumbled in her purse for the keys. One of the crew walked up and held out his hand saying, "Looking for these?" Kathy completely forgot she had given them up so her stuff could be loaded.

Sam leaned in through door for one more kiss good bye. You could see an almost tear in Kathy's eye once more as she saw the want and desire in Sam's. She really did not want to leave just yet, but knew she had to. Kathy waved as she drove off, looking in her mirror at Sam, standing there waving back. A sudden sadness fell upon Kathy, like she was never going to se him again. Sam watched until her car left the area, before going back into the hanger and into his office. Sam's first point of business was to call home, letting Shannon know they were back and everything went just fine.

Sam could tell, by the sound of Shannon's voice, that she was happy he was back. Shannon missed him knocking around the house all weekend. So, excitedly, she asked if he was going to be coming straight home or stopping off somewhere first on the way. Sam told her he was a little tired so he would be coming straight home after he hangs up. Sam sits down as he hangs up with Shannon. A last minute decision to check his mail was his next thought.

There were only a few, so he listened to them now instead of waiting till he got home and then would probably be too tired to listen. The messages were mostly from Rachael, letting him know about upcoming meetings and such. The last one however, was the same voice he had heard on Fri. This one was left this afternoon, shortly before they landed. The message told him to stay away from the meeting Monday. Puzzled, Sam thought to himself "Who knows that I was going to try and show up at the meeting? I only told two people and I'm sure neither of them were the caller. After all, one of them was with me on the plane." Sam looked to the floor, shook his head, while wondering what in the Blue Blazes is going on here.

Chapter 17

On the drive home, Sam quickly forgets about the call as his mind relives the weekends events. Kathy sure is becoming quite special he thought to himself. Yet deep down, there was something not setting right, something way too familiar about her. Like they really have met before or he's at least seen her before some where. Then he figured, why analyze? Just let things go and see where it takes him. After all, that's how he met up with his lovely wife. "Yeah that's it" Sam said aloud in his car while he drove, "Just let things happen as they may."

As Sam pulled into his driveway, he noticed that Shannon's car was not home. "Hmm, what a welcome home" he thought to himself. Sam didn't really dwell on it though as he parked and then went into the house. No sooner had he closed the door, he could hear a car pull up. Looking out the window, he saw Shannon had arrived home. Just to be funny, he waited by the door. Quickly, he threw it open as Shannon approached. "Welcome Home!!" Sam said yelled, with a smile. Shannon looked at him a little puzzled. "Oh wait! I'm the one that went away, yeah, that's it!"

Shannon did not really smile though as she walked passed him, saying "What ever! Did you have a nice time?" Puzzled, Sam replied "Yes, it was quite wonderful and fun and exciting and…." Shannon cuts him off in mid sentence saying "Well, I'm glad to hear you had fun. I need to get supper ready now." Sam was starting to wonder what was going on here. Shannon was not her usual self at all. "So" he continued, "Where did you go, what did you do while I was gone?" "Where!? What!? When!? Am I not entitled to a life too? You are not the only one around here with things going on and stuff to do." Shannon snapped and then sternly walked off in a huff to her room. Sam was not ready for the answer he was given.

He stood there for a minute, trying to figure this out, "She has never gotten mad like this before. She was sounding so happy when I talked to her on the phone a little bit ago." Sam decided to follow Shannon to her room. As Shannon closed her door, Sam stood there saying loudly "O.K. Let's talk. What has happened since I last talk to you on the phone?" he demanded to know. Total silence was all that Sam could hear. After a few minutes, the door slowly opened.

Shannon let the door swing open the rest of the way by itself. Sam stepped in and again asked the same question. This time, in a more softer tone. Shannon sat at the edge of her bed, took deep breath, then answered. "I didn't mean to snap like that at you, I'm sorry. I wanted to be home before you got there. I was getting a little something for your welcome home dinner and it fell through cuz the market was out. Then, I got a flat tier on the way home and then a ticket because I supposedly ran stop sign. So by the time I got home, I was a little ticked is all. I shouldn't have taken it out on you though, forgive me? Going to fire me now?"

Sam just shook his head as he sat beside her. Putting his arm around gently he replied, "Fire You!? Like I would let you off that easy. Nope, you're stuck here for ever now". Shannon continued to look at the floor. Sam bent down a bit to show the smile on his face, hoping it would cheer her up a bit. Shannon slowly started to grin as she saw the look upon Sam's face. Sam then added, "Tell you what, how about we go out tonight for a little bite? You seem to need a break and I think I do too. I mean the trip was really nice but there are just things that keep nagging at me. Perhaps a diversion will help me think better. O.K.?"

Shannon smiled even more now and said to Sam, "O.K., why not? Let me change real quick." As she stood up and walked toward her closet, Sam heard her say softly under her breath, in a mumble type voice "He just don't get it does he?" Sam ignored it however and left to room for Shannon to finish changing. As they drove to the restaurant, Sam told Shannon about the events and the show. When he got to the big payoff part, Shannon sat up straight, interrupting what Sam was telling her. "So, W-H-A-T did you do with the money?" she asked. "Oh let her keep it. It' not like I need it. Besides, she acted like a little kid in a candy store right after getting their allowance, Why?" Sam asked back, sort of puzzled. "Oh, no reason really. Just wondered." Shannon replies as she reaches to turn on the car radio as to not show her true feeling about it.

"Hey, this is one of my favorite songs!" Shannon tells him s she turns it up and then looks out the window. Shannon starts to think about the weekend and how much FUN he had and it started to get under her skin a bit. She knows she can't let him know how she feels because what if he doesn't feel the same? Then what? Certainly she can't tell him of her suspicions over Dear Ol' Kathy. What to do, what to do, she thought to herself.

Sam just drove the rest of the way, silently, until they got to the restaurant. "O.K., we're here. Let's eat." He said. "Gee, what a Romantic. It's no wonder you swept Kathy off her feet!" Shannon replied laughing. Relieved that Shannon seems to be in better spirits, Sam smiled too. After they entered and were seated, Shannon started to ask Sam if he was really interested in this lady or what. Sam told her that he was wondering that one himself. "Seems things just happen when ever she is around. I really can't explain it." He added. Shannon shook her head, took a deep breath and let it out. "O.K. look, do you know what her last name is by chance?" she then waited for an answer as Sam thought for a minute, then muttered "Ya know, I never asked."

Shannon, looking a little puzzled, could not figure how a guy could carry on and not even know the ladies full name. Shannon was now just aching to tell of her thoughts, of what she believed to be the truth about Kathy. None the less, she held her tongue and just changed the subject. "So, when are you two getting together again?" Shannon asked. Sam told her he is going to give her a call in the morning and take it from there.

Telling more of the weekend's events, Shannon had to say something before she exploded. Her mind seemed to be a total blank though. Sam picked up on the uneasiness in Shannon and asked. "Is there something I should know here? Come on now, you are more than a housekeeper to me and you know that, so tell me, what's up?" Sam asked sincerely, then placed his hand upon hers.

"More than that Huh?" Shannon Muttered. "Guess I'm just trying to watch out for you. Being MORE than a housekeeper, I guess it's why I care so much." Sam could tell she was not too comfortable talking about Kathy, even though it really made no sense at all as far as he could see. The subject was changed and they talked about work mostly and things around the house that need to be done. They talked all the way through dinner and dessert.

By the end of the evening, Sam and Shannon were feeling very relaxed when they left the restaurant to go back home. Not much was said on the ride home. Instead, they just listened to the radio. Sam and Shannon both got lost in their thoughts during the entire ride. The fact they both ate enough to feed a village could be a reason too as to why they just sat there quietly. As the headlights hit the driveway, Shannon snapped out of her little dream world and stretched a bit. Sam drove to the front door to let Shannon out, up close.

As Sam went to park the car in the garage, Shannon unlocked the house and went in. Shannon was already in her room and changing into her sleep attire, by the time Sam parked and came on in. Throwing on a robe, Shannon walked out of her room and down the hall There was Sam, standing by the door with a blank look on his face, keys in one hand and the bag of leftovers from the restaurant, in the other.

Shannon could tell he was still deep in thought. She has seen this face before, many times. "Amazing" she thought to herself "I'll never figure out how he goes from one mood to the other so quickly. Like someone just flipped a switch and it's a whole new person." She walked up to him, taking the bag from his hand. Shannon took a slow deep breath as she stepped a little closer to him, asking "You O.K.? You were all happy a second ago. Hit your head on the door or something?" she waited for an answer.

Sam just looked at her, with all the strange events that were running though his head once again, he replied "You said earlier you really cared and was not just as a hired help. You really ARE there for me aren't you?" Sam paused. Where this was all coming from Shannon had not a clue. In a caring voice she answered, "Yeppers, but I didn't think you really noticed much of that" With a smile, Shannon looked straight into Sam's eyes. Sam took a deep breath and managed a little smile. Without a word, he took her hands and gave them a gentle squeeze.

As he did this, he also kissed her on the forehead, concluding the night with saying, "We'll talk in the morning Darlin. I really am beat and I guess that's why I'm getting so quiet." Shannon, of course, didn't buy it for a second. She knew Sam all to well. Shannon knew something was up, but what? "O.K." was all she answered.

Sam let go of her hands and went on to his room, as so did Shannon. One last Good night was given as they each entered their room. Sam flipped the switch to turn on his light before closing his door. Slowly, Sam then walks to the side of the bed and turns on that light as well, returning to the door to turn off the main light.

Sitting on the edge of the bed, Sam kicks off his shoes and takes off his tie, then his shirt. He places his watch on the nightstand, then falls back, across the bed. As his body comes to a stop from bouncing, he thinks about Kathy, the trip, all the things that were said and done. His thoughts focused on the kisses she gave, the look on her face and how she would get so excited when she won.

The dancing too was thought of, as they would glide like they had done this for a long time, knowing each other's move, going with the music. He realized how alive she made him feel, how well she fit in his arms when he hugged her. It was as if... suddenly, Sam sat straight up, eyes wide open. With a blank look on his face, Sam quietly muttered, "Oh, My, God! Robin!" He stood up from his bed and placed one hand upon his forehead. Walking to his door and opening it to leave his room, Sam whispers to himself as he walks down the hall.

"No, no,,, this is, Stupid" He gets to the Bar in the den and pours himself a drink, straight up, no ice. He downs the first one in one huge gulp and pours a second to take back to his room. Shannon hears the commotion and steps out of her room to see what's up. As she sees Sam, now returning from the bar, she says, "I should have asked if you wanted a night cap, Sorry. I would have got it for you." "Well," Sam replies, "I just couldn't really unwind. I figured this would help perhaps." Shannon shows concern and asks if everything is O.K. Sam assures her that nothing is wrong that a good night's sleep won't cure.

Knowing better, Shannon does not push the issue but also does not believe what Sam is telling her. Shannon says OK and good night again as Sam slowly re enters his room and watches as he slowly closes his door.

Dangerous Secrets

Sam walks over to put his glass down on the nightstand, his mind going a million miles a second, he takes a small sip before going to the bathroom to finish undressing and getting ready for bed.

As Sam returns to the bed, he sits at the very edge. Just trying to relax and clear his thoughts. Sam picks up his drink quickly, but not as quick as the first one. With one swift move, the second drink is now finished. Placing the glass down slowly, he Pausing for just another second or two, then swings his legs over across the bed to lay down. Sam pulls the covers over him, takes a deep breath, exhaling slowly. Soon, Sam drifts off to sleep. He did not move a muscle, as he laid there. Dreams of Kathy and Robin, both danced in his head.

With a loud noise, the windows blew open, waking Sam from his sleep. The room grew cold, as a fog sort of rolled in across the floor. Sitting up with a start, from the nose, Sam notices a person standing in the corner of his room. He reached for the light, but it would not work. Sam called out Shannon's name softly, thinking perhaps it had been her. No answer was given. Not a sound was made as the silhouette seemed to float across the floor, getting closer and closer without a word being said.

Sam was starting to break into an icy sweet, when the figure held out a hand toward him, as if to say not to be alarmed and relax. Though Sam cold not tell who this was, he did not feel the least bit in danger or threatened. Swiftly yet slowly, the figure reached out it's hand to Sam. Sam sat motionless, not knowing what to do. He looked up at the figure that now stood before him, their face slightly covered with a veil. It wasn't till the figure spoke that Sam realized who it was. It was a very familiar woman's voice' it was the voice of his departed wife, Robin. "Please, I beg you dear. Leave the meeting alone. You will only be broken hearted once more. I'm sorry for what I've done and trouble I have caused you. Soon it will be morning and…." With a tear in his eye, Sam reached out, calling her name, wanting to ask what she was talking about.

The apparition did not finish what she saying, hearing the sound of someone knocking at Sam's bedroom door. As quickly as it appeared, it vanished. Shannon, not getting a response, entered the room quickly, rushing to his bed side. Sam was still sitting at the edge of his bed, staring off at the window. Shannon took a look in the same direction but could see nothing unusual. The wind was gently blowing in as she walked over to close them. Returning to Sam's bed side, She asked what he was calling for and what was the noise she heard.

"Bad Dream! Was all Sam answered. He then thanked her for closing the windows as he laid back down. Shannon offered to stay till he fell asleep, but Sam told her again, that everything is fine and that he was sorry for waking her. Shannon gently pulled the blanket up over Sam and said goodnight. As Shannon returned to her own room, Sam laid there, wondering if there would be a return visit or if it was indeed just a dream, he drifted off to sleep once more. This time there were no dreams of anything. Just a peaceful sleep.

Shannon however, was very concerned. She laid there all night, drifting in and out of one dream after another. There had to be an answer to all this, Shannon though, and she was determined to find it.

Chapter 18

Waking up early the next morning, Sam is not even thinking about the night he just went through. After getting dressed, Sam goes down stairs to the kitchen. He notices that he apparently has gotten up before Shannon, so he turns on the Coffee-pot then steps out the back door to get the paper.

Sitting down at the table to go over the news and assorted events, Shannon soon enters room, still half-asleep. Shannon does not notice right off that Sam is sitting at the table as she walks over to the coffee-pot. The aroma seems to pull her closer and closer. Smelling the brew, she grabs a cup, her eyes still half shut. Once she pours herself a cup she takes a little sip. As she does this, her eyes pop open, realizing she didn't make coffee this morning. Turning quickly, to face the table, she is started a bit to see Sam sitting there reading the paper. "Oh, You're up early this morning. Why didn't you say something when you saw me stumble on in here?" Shannon says, as she quickly closes her robe, hoping Sam saw nothing.

Sam lowers his paper slowly, then answers back "I didn't really sleep well last night. With all this cloak and dagger stuff going on. By the way, did you come into my room last night?" Shannon hesitated a bit before answering. "Yes I did, you were having some kind of dream and I went in to see what was going on. Don't you remember? Now, what would you like for breakfast?"

Sam sort of scratched his head and told her he sort of remembers a little of what went on but not much. Then, he tells her to make what ever she would like and that will be fine with him. It's her choice today. Shannon turns on the radio before getting breakfast ready. Sam is still buried deep in his paper, reading the business section.

Soon, Shannon serves up a plate, for both Sam and herself, then sits at the table to enjoy the meal. Shannon could tell there was more on Sam's mind than just the daily news from the paper. "So, a penny for you thoughts!" she asks lightly. "Aww, just thinking about Kathy is all and… Tell you what, how about you meet her first and then we'll talk about that subject" he tells her in response.

Cautiously, she asks him, "So, what is it I should know before meeting her? I mean, is there something in particular you want my opinion on?" A long pause came from Sam as he thought of an answer. "Hmm, since when did you, of all people, need a reason to give an opinion?" Sam says with a laugh and then adds, "I just want to see what you think of her in general is all."

Shannon smiles a bit, but knows there is there way more to this than Sam is letting on about. Trying not to think of it, she gets up from the table to clear the dishes. Shannon stops for a moment, looks over at Sam, and remarks "I'll just remember you said that." Turns and walks to the sink with an arm full of dishes.

Sam gets up chuckling, takes one last drink of coffee and then tells Shannon he will call from the office later, to let her know when and where to meet. Picking up his briefcase and keys, he tells Shannon good-bye as he heads out the door. Shannon watches from the window, hoping Sam will be O.K. and not worry to much about what all is going on.

Shannon knows that Sam usually lets things roll off, but this seems to really be eating away at him for some reason. Sam's drive in was as usual, no surprises. Once at the office, Sam finds Rachael already at her desk, she greets him with a smile saying. "Good Morning Sir!"

Looking back at her, Sam says without expression, "Well, it's a little too early to tell if it's going to be a good one or not, but after 10 this morning I will know for sure." With that, he walked into his office. Rachael wasn't too sure what to make over his comment, but did not waste a lot of time wondering. Sam walks over and places his briefcase upon his desk. Quickly he sits down and pulls out his weekly planner to see what dates are open for him.

The silence is soon broken with the sound of Rachael's voice over the intercom. "You have a call on line one, it's Kathy. Do you want to talk to her or shall I say you are not in yet?" Sam quickly tells her he'll take the call.

As soon as Sam picks up the phone to say Hello, he tried to tune out everything else. But no matte how he tries, his thoughts slowly turn to the 10am meeting. Kathy continued to talk until she realized he was not listening to a word she was saying. In mid sentence, to regain his attention, she said, "So then, after we shoot the video and let all the Midgets get dressed and go home we'll…"

Sam suddenly snaps back into reality, blurting out with, "What!? Video? Little People!? What the…." Kathy could hardly contain herself as quite loudly she starts to laugh. Amidst the laughing, Kathy did manage to say, "Oh, so you decided to listen now?" "I'm sorry." Sam replies "Just a lot of things on my mind these days. Let me make it up to you. How about dinner tonight, what do you say? Please?"

There was a short pause of silence before Kathy answered back. "Well, I suppose, but only if you are actually going to be there. Would you mind if my friend and her brother join us too this time? We could make a little party out of it." Sam quickly tells her the more the merrier since he was going to ask the same thing. He also adds that he knows of someone that might be a good date for her friend's brother. Kathy excitedly agrees, the time and place to get together later are quickly set.

Sam, now noticing the time, nicely puts an end to the conversation. He knows the he really needs to get to the meeting place. First, he looks through some papers before getting up to leave. He tells Rachael on his way out that he should be back shortly. Sam's goal right now is to get there and find a good parking spot, where he won't be noticed, but be able to see who this person is that's meeting with Bill.

As Sam gets to his car in the parking area, he notices a paper, stuck under his wiper blade. Thinking it's just another advertisement for something, he just casually takes it off. His eyes open wide though when he actually looks at it. It was note, written in bold print was, {YOU WERE NOT INVITED! DON'T EVEN THINK ABOUT IT!}. This did not detour Sam at all from going and hopefully getting some answers.

Sam, even more determined than ever, gets in his car and soon arrives at AMTRON. For a few minutes, Sam drove around to find just the right spot to park, in order to watch. Sam needed a spot that has a good view of the front of the building. Finding his spot, Sam settles in. He did not have to wait long before a car past him field of vision. The car that goes by has dark tinted windows, concealing who ever is inside. Sam sits still, watching carefully, as he is sure this must be the person.

Sam was on edge as he watched the person get out of their car. Sam started to think to himself that finally his questions will be answered. The person getting out of the car had their back to him, so he could not really see who it was. Sam watched as the person reached back into the car and pulled out a hat. It was a lady's, wide brim type, with the tie down sides. The person put on the hat, looked around real quick and then went into the building.

All Sam was able to find out for now, unfortunately, was that is was a lady. The rest of the mystery remains for Sam to try and solve. Deciding to wait a little more, Sam hopes to see the lady to come out, perhaps seeing her face this time. By 11:45am, Sam decided this waiting game has gone on long enough. But what excuse would he use to go up to Bill's office?

Chapter 19

As Kathy waited to see Bill, she thought about all the things she wanted to tell him and demand from him. She did not have to wait long before she was called in. Bill said Good Morning, cheerfully, but Kathy maintained a cold look upon her face. Glancing around the room before sitting down in front of Bill's desk, Kathy finally said "Hello. I suppose you are wondering why I am here." as she sat in front of him. Bill was more curious as to who she actually was.

Bills eyes opened wide, as if he'd seen a ghost, when he heard her say she was Robin's sister. Kathy continued "I'm here because I have all the shares in your company that were Kathy's. So, that would make me now a voice in this company's goings on." Bill interrupted, telling her that it's too late for anything now since it's going to be sold off. Kathy told him that she found that out when she got to the island but still it would not sway her in her plans at all. Bill asked very curiously as to what she meant by that, so Kathy began with the whole story of what she had been planning out over the last few years since her sister's death.

"First of all" She started "I was going to put you out of business, Since it's your fault my sister is dead." "Me!?" Bill asked sternly. "Yes! You!" Kathy answered and continued on "It's because of you that my sister is dead. Remember that night when one of your little rockets went a stray and blew up the car she was standing by?" Bill paused before answering. "Yes,,,,, I do.

But I wasn't anywhere around it when it went off and besides…" "Shut UP! Just shut the Hell up!" Kathy yelled. Taking a deep breath, she continued, "That rocket was meant for you, not her. I was there that night, she and I had planned the whole thing. You were out on your Yacht, watching the display. I was behind the scenes. I was supposed to tip the angel of the rocket toward your yacht. However, someone walked by at the last minute and I didn't get to finish. Before I could get back to it, it went it off."

Bill listened intently, as he felt a cold shiver through out his body. He couldn't believe what he was hearing. Kathy continued to tell of how her and Robin had set it up to look like an accident. Then, with all of Robin's shares, she would be in control. Robin's only crime was that she loved her husband very deeply. Didn't you notice how it just barely missed your boat as is flew on over it? I didn't know it had hit my sister's car till the next day. I ran off real quick after the launching." Kathy's eyes started to swell with tears as she relived what had happened. "Why are you telling me this now?" Bill asked. "I could have you arrested for this little confession ya know." Bill thought he had the upper hand now that this dumb broad had spilled her guts. Kathy regained her composer quickly and calmly said, "I don't think so!" as she pulled a gun out of her purse.

"Oh My God!" Bill stuttered, sitting there in his chair with that smug look on his face disappearing quickly. "Now,,, Now, we can talk about this!" "I'm done talking, Bill." Kathy said as she stood up and took a few steps toward Bill's desk. Not a word was spoken for a moment as Bill just stared at the cold steal of a barrel now pointed right him, only a foot away from his face. Bill did not make a move or even blink. Kathy's hand was very steady as she began to speak softly, in a very serious low tone. "I suppose I could do the world a favor and get rid of you, making it look like a suicide. They'll all just think you were under Corporate stress and did yourself in, out of depression of loosing your company. Happens all the time."

Bill tried to speak but Kathy shut him up with a cold stare and added "But I won't, not yet, maybe not ever, not sure yet what I'll do, but I know you WILL pay." Bill took a deep breath and then swallowed, sweat started to form on his brow and the side of his face. Kathy then told Bill that killing him would not bring her sister back but did want some kind of satisfaction. "None of this would have ever happened if you had not wanted to start up a little fun on the side. Robin only played along because of what you told her." "What are you talking about?" Bill said, hoping to throw her off track so he could grab the gun. Pulling back the hammer with a swift move, Bill heard the click and froze. He thought for sure he was going to be shot. "Give me a break!" Kathy said, with eyes cold as ice, "She told me that you found out about the stock she was buying and threatened to tell Sam it was actually for services rendered. Oh, but for an actual roll in the Hay you would not say anything about it. You played her like all the other women you've done. No matter what, she wasn't going to let you destroy Sam."

"Oh Please, she loved every minute of it!" Billed piped up, figuring if he's gong to be taken out, he might as well say something "She wasn't the least bit against the idea, full consent. You have nothing on me!" Besides, who would believe you anyway? So you got some Shares, big deal. That proves nothing." Trying to look calm and not afraid for his life right now, Bill starred back, as if the tables were now turning in his favor. Kathy shook her head and looked down just a bit, without taking her eye off Bill for even a second. With a little sarcastic tone in her voice, Kathy said calmly " Hmm, you are right, Bill. Suppose I could have gotten this stock anywhere. Gee, good thing I got the letters you sent her and copies of some of the responses she sent you. Oh and, of course let's not forget the Pictures I have of the two of you eating lunch and a few dinners together. OH, my Little Sis was no fool, She had all her bases covered. She figured she could use that to get you to keep quiet about telling Sam anything."

Bill looked at Kathy, calmly saying "So! What good is that now? My wife and I split up years ago. She's even remarried. Your little package of goodies is useless." Kathy laughed and pressed the gun to his head, "You really are stupid aren't you? Any court, anywhere, after I tell my story, will think you did indeed have her killed because you wanted her quiet. Wouldn't want dear wifey to find out and divorce you for everything you got. So the package is still good since you were married at the time of Robin's death. The way I see it, you have a choice, do as I say or you can try to talk your way out of this in jail. Any Questions?! Kathy turned her head slightly to one side as she waited for an answer.

Bill did not know what to think. His mind went blank except for the thought of that gun still in his face. Kathy lowered the gun slowly, saying she would shot him right now unless he gave her a reason. Putting the gun back in her purse she told him what she wanted. "I want you to do what ever it takes to make sure Sam gets the company. I know these stocks may not get me what I want right now, but I'll hang on to them till the deal is done. They'll be worth something again if the new owner wants to honor them. You just figure a way to leak the info to him about what it will take to outbid the others."

Exasperated, Bill exclaims "But they're sealed bids! How can I tell what Sam needs to bid?" Coldly, Kathy replied, "Gee, not my problem, Bill! Now is it?" Kathy started to turn to leave, but then stopped. She looked back at Bill, now standing behind his desk. "Oh, I wouldn't call security or anything, since I do have a license for my little peacemaker here. Doing that, will only ensure your jail time, when I turn over all that I have to the authorities. You're going down Bill, and Sam and I will both be laughing in the end."

Finishing her statement, she went straight for the door and left. Before leaving the building however, Kathy looked around carefully, in case Sam had indeed been there to try and see what this meeting thing was all about. Feeling secure that he was not around, Kathy went to her car and returned to where she was staying while on the Island. Kathy had no sooner entered the house when her friend started to give the third degree, firing question after question to find out how it went. Kristy danced around the number one burning question in her mind until she just blurted out "Did you shoot him or not?" Kathy looked at Kristy, no expression upon her face, coldly answer, "Why do you want to know?" Kristy became very scared. Kathy sat at the Kitchen table. A big grin started to grow upon Kathy's face after a minute or two of silence. Kristy didn't know what to make out if it.

Kathy then told her the truth "No, I didn't shot the poor bastard, though I did want to. Bill is still unfortunately breathing. Kristy began to breathe again after hearing Bill was not dead. "You little Shit! Don't scare me like that" she told Kathy, with a slightly mad tone, as she sat at the table with Kathy. "So? Tell me what did happened then." Kristy added.

Kathy began to tell her the whole sorted story of what happened and what little Bill had to say. Kristy tried once more to warn Kathy about what she was doing and to be careful. "I know what I'm doing, don't worry." Was all Kathy told her as she quickly changed the subject. Before she could

Dangerous Secrets

say much though, the phone rang, Kristy got up to answer it. After saying Hello, she looked at Kathy and then handed the phone to her, saying with mysterious type tone to her voice to be funny "It's Him!" Kathy slowly said Hello, wondering who it was, yet hoping it would be Sam.

As she heard the voice on the other end say "Hello Darlin!" Kathy eyes lit up a bit, it was Sam. He called to tell her about the little dinner get together, also inviting her friend and friend's brother. Sam went on to tell her that Shannon would be there too, since she is single, perhaps her friend's brother would like to meet her. Kathy got a little quiet when she heard Shannon was going to be going. She knew she could not back out and give Sam a good reason.

Kathy just hoped her sister didn't tell Shannon too much about what was going on or talked about her dear ol' sister Kathy, let alone showed her pictures! A lot of things quickly went through Katy's mind as her heart started to race a little from the possible outcome of the dinner. Sam picked up on this short silence and asked if things were OK. Kathy thought quick, telling him everything was fine, she was wondering what to wear tonight is all and if Adam and Shannon would like each other. Sam, then continued to tell her about the time and location and not to worry about Adam and Shannon.

Kathy's face grew a little worried as she hung up. Kristy asked too if everything was ok or not. Kathy's answer to her was a little different than the one she just gave Sam. Telling Kristy of Shannon's being there too, Kristy asked "Well, do you think Shannon will know who you really are when she sees you? "I don't know." Kathy replied "Sis never did say anything about Shannon knowing about any of this or that she saw pictures or anything. I really don't know what to think."

Kristy just sat there with a look of concern on her face as Kathy walked out of the room, going up to her Bedroom to lay down and think for a few moments. As Kathy laid there, thinking, thoughts of Sam and the weekend started to filter through. Reliving for a moment the fun and excitement they had shared. Starting to feel a little guilty for the first time in her life, Kathy decided to go through with the dinner and not try to come up with some excuse as to not being able to attend. Kathy figured she would take her chances.

Kristy entered the room after a bit and walked up to Kathy, giving her a little nudge to let her know she has been asleep now for a few hours now and really should be getting up to get ready for tonight. Katy stretched and rubbed her eyes a bit. "Gee, guess I was more tired than I thought" She told Kristy. Kristy started to walk out of the room as Kathy got off the bed, headed straight for the bathroom to cleanup and get ready. "Let me know if you need anything!" Kristy yelled as she left the room.

Chapter 20

As Kathy finished in the shower, Kristy knocked on the door and told her there was a phone call for her. "Be out in a minute!" Kathy shouted through the door. Rubbing her hair with a towel, Kathy went and sat on the edge of her bed to answer the phone. "Hello?" Kathy's temper rose just a little when heard the voice on the other end. "Hey Kat, how'd it go? I really couldn't wait till you got a round to call me so I figured I'd call you." Kathy's voice was stern as she replied "Everything went well I suppose. I told you I would get in touch later and never to call me here. What the hell are you thinking?" "Oh relax." The voice replied "no one knows who I am and besides, you can always just say it was someone from dear ol' Sam's office calling you about something."

Kathy took a long pause and told him she would call him back later, when no one was around. The caller though, would not accept that, demanding to meet with her, tonight. She tried to explain that it would not be possible, due to a little dinner party. The caller quickly add in that he could always find out where she was going to be tonight and just show up. Kathy got a bit nervous over this little threat and decided that it may best to meet before her dinner tonight. They agreed on a meeting place and Kathy hung up slowly, trying to figure out why it was so important to meet tonight.

Soon though, she put it out of her mind and picked out what to wear for the evening. Suddenly, Kathy felt a coolness sounding her. She looked over at the window but it was not open, the AC seemed to not be blowing either. A strange feeling came over her. Not being able to explain it, Kathy chalked it up to being so concerned over meeting the caller tonight. Carrying her outfit to the bathroom, Kathy's face ran cold and pale. She dropped the outfit and just stared at the mirror, still a little steamed up from her shower. On the mirror was a message, written in the fog covered glass. "Don't Hurt Him!" was all it said and the letter "R" appeared at the end, just under the sentence.

Kathy could hardly move, as she read it over and over again. As the message faded with the fog, she stopped shaking and walked toward the mirror, hesitantly. Placing a hand where the writing was, Kathy very softly whispered "Robin?" She recognized the hand writing as it was sort of unique in its style. Still a bit shaken, Kathy turned and went back to pick up her clothes and then walked over to the bed. She sat with a thud, like her legs had just suddenly gave out. Staring ahead with no thought really going through her mind, Kathy stood up and dropped her robe to the floor, proceeding to get dressed.

Trying not to pay too much attention to the message, Kathy put on a little make-up and brushed out her hair. Soon, she was ready to leave. As she walked into the living room, she saw Kristy sitting on the couch, watching T.V. Kristy glanced up and said "Gee, you look dressed to kill." Kathy was wearing a mid length navy blue skirt that had a split up one side, smoked black hose and high heels to match the skirt. Her blouse was white and sort of low cut with a ruffle front and long sleeves.

Kathy walked over and sat in the chair next to the couch. She then asked if Kristy had gone in her room at all while she was drying her hair with the towel. Kristy gave her a funny look and asked why. Kathy made up an answer about thinking she heard someone walk in but didn't see anyone. Kathy then changed the subject, telling Kristy she would be leaving a little sooner than she thought before meeting up with Sam.

Kristy, being a quick thinker, asked "Something to do with the phone call?" Kathy remember what the caller had said, so she told Kristy, "It was just someone from Sam's office asking what I'll be wearing tonight because Sam has a little surprise for her later." Kristy was not sure if she should buy this little story she was being told. Tilting her head a little, Kristy answered back "O.K. just be careful and call if you need anything." Kathy smiled and said she was sure she could handle what ever Sam has in mind. Picking up the keys on her way out of the house, Kathy said good night as she closed the door behind her.

On her way to her first little stop, Kathy called Sam from her cell phone, explaining she had to run by the store to pick something up before dinner, so it will be better to just meet with him at the Restaurant instead of him picking her up. Sam was not real happy about the change in plans and offered to wait for her till she got back. Kathy was firm about her decision and said to please just let her meet them all there instead. Sam thought for a moment then gave in reluctantly. Kathy said thank-you and hung up the phone.

After a few more minutes, she arrived at the meeting point but did not see her appointment any where in sight. Kathy started to wonder if this was a set up or what. Just then, headlights came up from behind her. A white car pulled up and stopped, it was the same car that had been following Sam around the island. A middle aged gentleman got out and walked over to Kat, still sitting in her car. Kathy could see in her rear view mirror who it was, so she got out of her car quickly to see what he wanted so bad and get on with her evening.

"Hello" he said as he walked on over, his arms outstretched for a hug. "Just tell me what you want. I'm kind of in a hurry." Kathy said while brushing off the hug. "Calm down" he said, "You have time. I just want to know if Bill understood what we want is all. I need some confirmation that you are not trying to stab me in the back too. I know how you play, so I figure I need to be on top of things." Kathy thought for a moment before answering.

"Look, I've changed my mind and want no part of the company anymore." What? You little….." he started to say before getting interrupted by Kathy "Don't worry, and don't you EVER call me that! Bill will be calling you, I'm sure, to let you know what the price is, figuring that you will tell Sam. Then you can buy him out or what ever and take over. The problem is going to be Sam though, if you keep running around like that and letting him see you, you'll blow everything. Sam is no idiot." "Yes, I know. I had to think quickly the other day when he questioned me about some stuff. Just call me later tomorrow so we can set up the rest of this little take over." He added.

Kathy agreed and started to get back in her car, before she could, he grabbed her arm to get her to look at him. His eyes stared into her's. There was a cold look upon his face, "Don't even try to screw with me on this, you won't like the out come, Kat." He then released her arm, letting her continue to get in her car and drive off. Kathy was quiet angry over how he had talked to her and thought to herself that maybe she should be the one looking out for a knife in the back. She started to picture Sam's face as she drove off to meet with him, soon her anger turned to a relaxing feeling. Kathy is starting to realize that she is falling for Sam and this really would not be a good thing at all.

As she drove up to the Restaurant and parked, Kathy looked around for Sam's car but did not see it anywhere in sight. Slowly, Kathy got out and walked into the restaurant, asking if Sam had made it yet. The Host told her he had not yet made it in and would she like to wait at the bar. Kathy agreed, thinking a good stiff drink would do her some good right now to calm her down a bit and keep her in a good mood. She went in to the bar area and ordered. Sitting there, she started to think of her sister, the plan, the set up, how things seem to be getting a bit intense, What her next move should be and so on.

Chapter 21

As Sam arrived home from work, Shannon greeted him with questions about what to wear for tonight's little get together. Sam thought for a moment and asked if she wanted him to dress her as well, then he smiled. Shannon quickly said in reply "Ummmm, no! One thing would lead to another and then you would fall in love and I would fall asleep!" Shannon then let out with a big laugh as she turned to go to her room. Sam chuckled on his way to his room as well. Before long, Sam came down stairs, dressed in a nice casual suite and tie. Shannon put on a slim fitting dress that really showed off every curve. When Sam looked at her, he was at a loss for words. "What?" Shannon asked "My slip showing or something?" Stuttering a little, Sam remarked about the low neck line this dress had, or the lack of a neck line all together.

"Why Sam!" Shannon exclaimed "You've seen more than this before when you've walked out to the pool while I was laying there. If I didn't know any better, a girl would think you were having ideas or something." With a little shy girl look in her eye, Shannon looked at Sam, waiting for an answer. "Well, I just didn't want this guy to get the wrong impression of you." "GUY!? What Guy?" Shannon's tone turned serious as Sam told her about the Brother of Kathy's best friend. Shannon didn't know if she should yell at him for setting her up with a date or just leave it as is and see what all happens.

After all, she did wear this for Sam, not some guy she was going to meet. "Just wished you would have told me is all." Shannon finally remarked. "We have a few minutes to kill yet." Sam uttered. "Kathy called me earlier today and told me she had an errand to run before meeting tonight and that she would just me there instead of me picking her up this time." Shannon looked a little puzzled and asked Sam what the errand was. Sam said he didn't ask her, so he did not know. This made Shannon even more suspicious. After a few more minutes of idle talk, the two went off to the car to join the rest at the restaurant.

As they drove, Shannon told Sam that she didn't know what all he wanted her to be looking for as to what he was hoping to find out. Sam assured her there was no hidden meaning to this dinner or that he hoped to find out anything really. He just wanted to get Shannon's opinion and that she should just act like herself, no big mystery. Shannon of course, agreed and said she would just take what ever as it comes and give a full report before bedtime. Sam's happiness is all that matters to Shannon, so she hoped her own feelings would not get in the way.

With this in mind, Shannon, point blank, asked Sam "What if I don't like this lady? What if I think you can do better or that I feel she may be up to something? Then what? Tell you the truth? Will you listen to me if I do?" Sam shook his head a bit and answered "I didn't say I was thinking of marrying this lady, I just wanted to see what you think about her is all. So yes, Please do be honest and tell it like you see it. That's why I set this thing up, I know YOU will be honest with me no matter what."

By now, they had reached their destination and parked the car. Sam got out first and decided to be the Gentleman, opening Shannon's door. By the time Sam got around the car though, Shannon was already out. "Don't give a guy a chance do ya?" Sam said with a little laugh. "Snooze ya loose buddy!" Sam just looked at her with a smile and extended his am to escort her in. This clued Shannon that Sam was not acting himself tonight. Sam had never tried to open a door for her or escort her like that. Shannon knew this would be and interesting evening of events.

As they entered, the Host quickly came up to greet them. Sam said they were supposed to be meeting someone there. When Sam told him who it was and gave a slight description, the Host knew right away where the lady was sitting and took both, Sam and Shannon to the bar. Kathy's back was to the entrance so she did not see Sam walk up. As she was taking a drink, she caught Sam in the corner of her eye. Kathy finished her drink with one quick swallow and turned as she placed the glass down upon the bar.

As she hopped down off the bar stool, her arms reached out to give him a hug, then noticed another lady standing next to him. "Oh. Hello." Kathy said. Sam started to introduce Shannon to Kathy, before he could finish though Kathy cut in with a little humor "I know who this is, since I didn't want you to pick me up you brought along a replacement, in case I didn't show up at all Huh?" Sam wasn't sure what to think due to Kathy's straight face, acting like she was serious. After a quiet moment, Kathy finally broke a smile, saying, "Naw, I'm just joking. This must be your lovely housekeeper Shannon, I've heard so much about. My Friend and her brother are not hear yet but lets get a table anyway to wait for them."

Shannon could tell Kathy had perhaps had more than one drink while waiting for them to show up. Sam did not notice the same thing at first, until the Host lead them to the table and Kathy started to walk a little on the crooked side. Before they all sat down, Shannon gave Sam a little tap to get his attention, whispering in his ear that she wanted to talk to him real quick. Sam made up an excuse to Kathy in order to leave the table and walk off. Shannon said she had to go the restroom and would be right back.

Sam and Shannon met up on the other side of the bar, out of Kathy's view completely. "Sam!" Shannon started "What on earth are you thinking? You said to be honest and I'll tell ya, I don't like this so far at all. She's already drunk and the dinner has not even started yet." Sam cut in to assure her that Kathy is not like this normally, so to please see past that and just try to have a good time.

Shannon sort of rolled her eyes at the thought of all this and also because of the blind date she was fixed up with. Shannon quickly put on a smile though and returned to the table. As Sam was about to go to the table too, he heard a man's voice ask about Kathy, up front. Sam went to see who it was and saw a man a young lady standing there talking to the Host. Quickly, Sam walked up and asked "Adam, Kristy?" Kristy spoke first "Why yes. You must be Sam?" Sam held out his hand as Kristy shook hands with him and Adam did the same while introducing himself.

Kristy was all smiles and ready for a party as Sam lead them to the table. Adam was about as nervous as could be since he was told only moments before entering that he was going to be meeting a lady tonight. Seems Shannon and Adam both were a little in the dark till now. Once at the table, Sam introduced Adam and Kathy to Shannon. Shannon sort of raised an eyebrow of approval when she laid eyes upon Adam. Adam too, suddenly had a little gleam in his eye. Adam thought Shannon was quit beautiful and Shannon had the same thoughts about Adam, being very cute. Both were hoping this would be an omen, for the date to no turn into a Blind Date From Hell!

As they all sat and the evening began, Sam asked Kathy if she got the stuff she needed ok. Kathy looked puzzled at first and then remembers the story she told him as to why she would meet him there instead of being picked up. "Oh yes, I got what I wanted" Kathy remarked. Soon, a waiter came to take the drink order. Kathy ordered a Slow Gin Sour. Shannon didn't think much of it really but it did sort of stick in her head for some reason.

As the dinner progressed, Shannon became more and more uneasy. Certain words Kathy would use and the way she looked, reminded Shannon more and more of Robin. The questions got a little more personal from Shannon, in hopes to find her answer as to why she felt this way.

"So, Kathy, where are you from originally, could it be Texas?" Shannon asked. "Why yes." Kathy replied, "South Texas. Why?" "Oh, just some of the words you used is all. Sounded like someone else I knew that came from Texas." Sam stared to wonder what Shannon was up to with her questioning. Just then, the Band started up, breaking the line of questioning. Adam stood up from the table and turned his attention to Shannon. "Excuse me, but I believe they are playing our song dear lady. Would you care to join me on the dance floor?" Shannon thought for a second but could not refuse such a gallant offer. Shannon took Adams hand and got up from the table. The whole time though, she could not really take her eyes off of Kathy. Something was just not sitting right in Shannon's mind about Kathy. Kathy picked up on this and became a bit nervous, she felt as though Shannon was looking right through her.

As Adam and Shannon entered the dance floor, Sam took Kathy's hand and asked what was on her mind. "Nothing really" Kathy started to tell Sam, "It was just that look on Shannon's face, when I said I was from

Texas. It was like she saw a ghost or something." "Well." Sam explained, "Remember I told you I had a wife that died? Robin was from Texas so it probably brought up some memory. I'll talk to her later, don't worry yourself about it all. Now, Wanna join them on the floor?" Kathy looked over at Kristy for a second and then back at Sam. "I think you and Kristy should dance a little and get to know each other better. I need to give my dinner time to settle first."

Kristy smiled while looking up at Sam, saying "That would be a good idea!" Quickly, Kristy stood up, taking Sam's hand she sort of pulled him on the dance floor before he cold say anything. Kathy sat watching, thinking and wondering if Shannon knew her or not. As Sam danced with Kristy, he asked how she and Kathy had met. "We were room mates back in college. After graduation, I moved to the Island here and she went off abroad to find her fortune in the art world so to speak." Kristy told Sam. "So, you've lived her long then?" Sam asked. "About 7 years I guess now. I haven't seen much of Kathy though till lately. It's always nice to see an old friend ya know." Sam agreed as they kept on dancing. He looked over at the table and say Kathy looking a them on the floor. He gave a little smile and wink to Kathy and Kathy returned the gesture to Sam.

When the music stopped, Sam and Kristy returned to the table. Shannon and Adam though, stayed out there for the next number. As Adam looked at Shannon, standing close in his arms, he could sense something was on her mind. Looking down and puling back just a bit, Adam said, "Penny for your thoughts!?" Shannon looked up and took a deep breath. "I'm sorry" Shannon stated "It's just been a long day is all. So, you and Kristy are from Texas too?" Shannon asked. Adam chuckled and told her that he and Kristy were from Wisconsin actually and that Kristy had met Kathy in College.

"What, uh, College did They go to?" was Shannon's very next question. Adam thought for a moment and then told her it was A.S.U. Shannon became very quiet now as all the pieces seem to fit in, believing she now knew who Kathy was really was. But the one question remained, Why didn't she just tell Sam who she was instead of all this mystery? And, should she tell Sam who she believes Kathy to be? Would he believe her? A Million more questions now went through Shannon's mind.

Chapter 22

As the music stopped once more, Shannon and Adam returned to the table to take a breather. As they sat down, Kathy commented how cute the two of them looked out there on the dance floor. Shannon said thank-you as Adam looked over at Shannon. "I think so too" Adam commented and then asked if he could see her again sometime. Shannon wasn't sure what to say right off, so she told him she would think about it. Kathy was hoping the two of them would hit it off better.

By now, it was getting a little late and Kathy was definitely feeling the effects of the drinks. Sam suggested they call it an evening and offered to see Kathy home. Sam also asked if Adam could drive her car for her. Adam agreed to do this. Kathy looked at Sam with half glazed eyes and though to herself "What a sweet and considerate guy you are." Kristy piped up and told Sam she could drive dear old Kathy back to the house. Sam didn't mind doing it but thought it might be a good idea since Shannon would have to be going along too. "OK." Sam replied, "As long she gets home safe." Kathy said nothing since she was a bit more than just relaxed. Maybe it's just the drinks talking but Kathy believed tonight, that she indeed was falling for Sam and that was not in the plans at all.

Sam held her by the arm and around the waste as he guided her to the car. After he helped her sit inside, Sam gave her a kiss a goodnight. Adam had escorted Shannon to her car and helped her in. Pausing for a moment, Adam asked her again if they could meet sometime. Shannon agreed and told him he could get the number from Kathy later. Feeling quite good about this, Adam leaned in for a kiss. Just before there lips met, Shannon did a quick little head turn and Adam ended up kissing her on the cheek instead. He did not comment though and simple said Good-night.

Sam reached the car as Adam closed the door for Shannon. As Adam walked away, Sam commented as he got in, "So, are you two going to go out sometime? What did you think of him?" All Shannon said as she stared out the window was "He's OK I guess. I might go out sometime. Not sure though. Time will tell. All things in their own time.." Sam interrupted, "Hello? What are you talking about? I asked a simple question is all."

Shannon snapped out of her little trance and looked over at Sam. "Oh, I'm sorry. Didn't mean to ramble like that. Guess its just one too many drinks tonight for me too." Sam smiled and changed the subject to Kathy, asking what Shannon thought of her. Shannon thought for a minute before answering with her true thoughts. She knew she couldn't tell Sam what she believed to be true without a little more proof yet or if she should tell him at all and if so, how? A million questions went through Shannon's head in a split second as she thought of an answer to give Sam.

"Well, Gotta be honest with ya. She reminds me of someone for sure and….." Sam stopped her cold by cutting in with, "Now don't start with the Robin theory again. I know she has few things about her that are the same but don't you think there could be someone with the same good qualities as Robin had?" Shannon reached over and put her hand on Sam's shoulder gently. "I was going to say," she continued "That though she reminds me of someone, it is NOT Robin. There's just something familiar about her is all. She seems like a nice enough lady, I just don't want you get burned is all. Is it a crime to care? You Did ask me to be honest so don't get all defensive on me here."

Sam took a breath and apologized for jumping on her like that and agreed that he did indeed tell her to be honest and she was doing just that. The rest of the ride home was a little quiet, as the only thought that was going through Shannon's head right now is what box in the attic were the old Photo Albums being kept? Pictures are worth a thousand words and don't lie, this would tell if she was or not, Robin's sister. Soon, the two arrived home and went on into the house. Sam tossed the keys on the counter and headed for the living room to sit for a minute or two to relax. Kicking off his shoes, Sam looked around but didn't Shannon anywhere in sight.

"Odd." He thought to himself "She was right behind me. I thought for sure she would have sat right down and gave the third degree about Kathy." Sam leaned back on the couch and closed his eyes. While he rested there, Shannon had gone up to the attic and started to look at boxes, quietly. She didn't want Sam to hear her and come up wondering what was going on. After looking through two boxes, the third one she hit pay dirt. It was full of old photos that had been packed away now for a few years. Sam never wanted to see them again after the terrible night on the 4th of July.

As Shannon quickly went through one album after another, she came upon one labeled "FAMILY" "This is it!" She said quietly to herself. As she turns each page, memories of happier days came back to her. Half way through the book, there is was, a picture of Robin, dressed real nice, with her sister standing next to her wearing her cap and gown from College graduation. Though it was a few years old, Kathy had not changed a bit. Now, the question was, how to get this in front of Sam so he will see it. Shannon knew the bold approach would be to pull out the picture and hand it to him.

Shannon thought that would be a bit cold though and finally decided to leave the book in the attic for now, on top of the box it was found in. Later, she would bring it down and put it someplace that Sam would see, perhaps taking a look again after all these years. That way, he would find the picture on his own. Shannon left the attic, hoping Sam was not looking for where she went. Quietly, she went down the stairs and looked around to see if Sam was near by. Not seeing him anywhere in sight, she made her way quietly to her room and began getting for bed.

Sam had started to stir a bit and got up from the couch to head off to bed himself. As he walked past Shannon's room, he noticed the light was still on and the door slightly open. Curious as to why she didn't come to sit and talk, he walked up to the door and looked in. Before he cold call her name, he saw her standing in the bathroom that was off to the side of her room, catching her image in the mirror. Shannon had her hands up in the air as she was pulling off her dress.

Sam couldn't help but watch this little show. As the dress came off, slowly sliding up her body, Sam saw the silk, dark blue thong she was wearing. Then, as the dress came to the top, he saw her fine bare breast. Shannon turned as the dress came off and didn't see Sam's reflection in the back ground. Feeling a little guilty about peeking in like that, Sam ducked his head back quickly and called her name from the hallway, like he was just getting to her room. Shannon quickly grabbed her night shirt to slip it on.

"Yes?" Shannon answered back. "I was just wondering why you didn't come and sit and talk with me?" Sam continued. Shannon now walked to the door way and told him she already said what she thought and was really tired so she went on to her room. With the image in Sam's mind of her standing there in the mirror, his eyes never really looked directly at her. Shannon noticed this, remarking. "What's wrong? You keep looking away." Sam had to think of something fast, "I'm just tired is all and the light from your room seems to hitting just right at this angle in my eyes"

Shannon believed what Sam told her. Saying Good-Night, Sam went straight to his room and closed the door. After taking his clothes off, he laid them across the chair in the corner. Sam walked on over and slipped into bed. After Sam turned off his light and closed his eyes, The image of Shannon was still very vivid. He thought that to be a bit strange, "I've seen little things like that before, here and there over the years so why is it lingering like this? He thought to himself. Sam dismissed it after a minute or two of thinking about it, playing little mental guy games in his head about the "What If's" of her being naked. Quickly, Sam fell deep asleep. The dream he was about have though was not like anything he had ever had before.

Chapter 23

As the night continued and Sam lay there sleeping, Shannon looked out her door and down the hallway toward Sam's room. Seeing no light on from under his door, she silently crept by his room to the attic again. Ever so slowly, Shannon opened the attic door, went in, and retrieved the photo album. As quietly as she entered, Shannon left the attic and went down the hall to the den. Looked for just the right place to put the album, Shannon saw a spot on the bookcase. There were some old books there that didn't look like they had been touched in a long time.

Placing the there, she thought to herself "Some time tomorrow, when he gets home from work, I'll come on in here and pretend to be looking for a book and suddenly run across this one. I'll place it….over there,, to get it out of my way after I mention it to him. Yeah, that's it!" With a smile now, Shannon leaves the room and again quietly creeps back to her room and closes the door. With a sigh of relief for pulling it off with out a hitch, Shannon went to her bed and settled down for a good night's sleep.

While Sam slept, he started dream. He dreamt of himself standing on his boat, all alone at night. The Boat was a drift in the water. Though there was not a cloud in the sky, not a single star could be seen. There was only a single light, seemingly coming from the distant shore. Slowly a fog rolls in across the water. It does not cover over the boat like a normal fog. It seems to wrap itself around the base of the boat, continuing on past. A fog horn is heard in the far distance along with the ring of a bell as well. From out in the distance, comes a small row boat with two figures being carried in it approaches.

One, is the figure of a man wearing a cloak with a hood over his head. Sam watched as this person continued to row, getting closer and closer. Not showing any signs of slowing, Sam called out to warn them that they were about to hit Sam's boat. Just then, the other figure, also dressed the same, stood up in the boat and answered back "Do not worry, he will stop." As the little row boat came with in inches of Sam's boat, it came to a dead stop, no drifting or any movement at all. It was like it suddenly hit land.

He could not see the face of the person standing, but knew by the voice, it was a lady. "May I board?" The lady asked without looking up at Sam while reaching out one hand. Sam was not sure what to think of this yet felt compelled to let the lady board. Sam said nothing as he reached out to help her up on to his boat. "Thank-you" She said. She stood there with her arms folded into her extremely large sleeves that were part of her robe.

Sam stood right in front of her as she kept her head bowed. He asked who she was and waited for answer. The figure started to talk but stopped after only two words "I Need….." One of her hands then came out and moved up to the hood, pulling it back as she finished her statement "I Need to talk to you!" As the hood uncovered the face, Sam grew cold. Sweat formed on his face, Sam grew a little pale as he stared into the eyes of this ever so beautiful woman he knew as his wife, Robin.

Sam was speechless as he stood motionless before her. She looked every bit as beautiful as he remembered during these lonely years apart. Sam reached out to touch her, but she pulled back quickly, telling him "No, I need to talk." Sam offered to go sit in the cabin and she agreed. As they sat down, Sam was a bit shaky as Robin began. "I have so much to tell but no time to tell it. Just know that I watch over you and miss you greatly. I did love you and always will. I didn't realize how much though till I past away. Please forgive what you are about to find out and don think ill of me. I really NEED to hear you say you will forgive me, when you find out."

Sam had not a clue as to what she was talking about. Desperately, he tried to get her to explain better. All Robin would say now was, "I Love you, Forgive me, Please?" Over and over she said this, till Sam agreed and promised that no matter what it is she is talking about, he would forgive it all. He saw a tear start to come from Robin's eye, then another right after. Sam reached to wipe the tear away, Robin pulled back quickly, but not quick enough his hand seemed to go through her. Sam gasped in fear sitting a little further back in his seat.

"What the…???" He started to say as Robin put one finger to her lips, asking that he be silent and not to worry. Robin then reached under her robe and slowly pulled out a book. It was an old Photo Album marked "FAMILY". She placed it on the table before Sam, instructing him to look at it, also to remember to forgive. "Forgive what?" He kept asking. No answer would be given though. The sound of a second bell now was heard. Robin stood up quick and pulled the hood back over her face and told him she must leave now.

Sam tried to stop her, but could not. He started to beg and pleaded that she take him with her. The tears flowed down Sam's face as he watched helplessly. Robin was leaving him once again. Hearing the tearful cry, Robin stopped, turned slowly and looked as Sam. "We will be together again one day." She said. "But not now. You have so much to live for yet and do." Robin's love was still strong and though she had to go, she walked back over to him and told him to close his eyes. Sam did as he was instructed. Robin then placed a warm tender kiss upon his lips.

Sam kept his closed as she stopped and turned to walk away once more. After a few seconds, Sam opened his eyes once more and watched as she walked back into the boat that brought her. Before she sat down, she looked up at Sam one last time. Seeing the tears still streaming from his face, she too started to cry. "YOU cannot go with me, it's not your time. But I shall never leave you, I shall live in your heart and memories, as well as your dreams for as long as you will allow. I'm sorry Sam, I'm so VERY SORRY For all I did. I LOVE YOU!!!"

AS Robin stopped talking, a third bell was heard. It rang louder than other two and the man still sitting in the boat, started to row. Sam watched the little boat row toward a light that seemed to be was coming from the shore. He wanted to jump in and follow, but he found that he could not move. Continuing to look at the boat, he could see Robin was still standing, looking back at him. Sam took a deep breath, deeper than he though he could ever do and yelled with all his heart and soul, "I LOVE YOU ROBIN!!!!!! I ALWAYS WILL AND I WILL FORGIVE AND KEEP YOU FOREVER IN MY HEART!!!!"

After Sam yelled those words, Robin waved one hand in recognition that she heard him. Just before the boat slipped out of sight, Sam heard one more time, softly "I Love you Sam!" The boat now completely out of sight, Sam fell to his knees and cried. Looking up at the dark night he yelled "Why???? WHY!!!!!!???" Sam bowed his head for a moment before he slowly got up and headed back into the cabin. As he sat at the table again, he looked at the album sitting there in front of him.

Reaching out slowly, he picked it up and hugged it against his chest, thinking about Robin. After a minute, Sam placed the book back down on the table and closed his eyes. With in what seemed to be only a second, Sam's eyes opened wide from an uneasy feeling. There, standing over him, was a figure that words could not describe. A cold freezing shiver ran though his body as he stared up at the thing standing there. The creature standing before him seemed to have smoke and fire raising off it's shoulders. It stood at least 8 foot tall and spoke in a deep gruff voice. It told Sam "You will not be looking in that book and to make sure of this, I am taking it away. She had no business giving it to you and you do not need to know!"

Sam quickly grabbed the book. The hideous looking figure grabbed for it at the same time. Sam saw it's long fingers, twisted and bruised looking. It's hands had long pointed finger nails and patches of cores dark hair. It grabbed strongly on to the book, trying to free it from Sam's grip. Sam would not let go, saying he would die before he would give it over. The creature now started to laugh, saying "That can be arranged!" Just then, a light flooded the cabin and the creature turned his head away quickly.

"Let Go!" came a voice from outside the cabin. The voice was loud and did not sound like anyone Sam knew. Sam fell back on the bench as the beast let loose, fleeing from the cabin in a rush. Sam looked down at the book, still tightly clutched in his hands. As he slowly started to open it, Sam suddenly woke from his dream, sitting straight up in his bed. A cold sweat covering his body, his breathing was strong and deep. Quickly he looked around and saw he was back in his own room. Sitting very still, Sam gathered his thoughts and then relaxed, allowing his head to fall back on the pillow. He rolled to one side, ever so softly calling out Robin's name one more time before he fell back to sleep.

Chapter 24

As Sam woke up the next morning by the sun shinning through his window, he still felt a bit shaken from the dream. Trying to clear his thoughts and shake it off, he swung his legs over the edge of the bed to sit up. Ever so slightly, he felt his leg brush against something that was hanging over the edge of his nightstand. He looked to see what it was. Laying there on the edge of his little table, he noticed a book, it was a Photo Album with the label "FAMILY" on it. Sam started to recall the entire dream now. Causing him to be a bit hesitant in picking it up, let alone touch it. Slowly, Sam reached out and picked up the book. Without opening it, he placed it back down and got up to put on his robe.

Snatching up the book again, he headed down to the kitchen where he hoped to find Shannon like he always does, first thing in the morning. Sure enough, there was Shannon, busy making a great breakfast like usual. The coffee smell was filling the air as it brewed, Shannon did not see or hear Sam come into the kitchen. "Well." Sam said loudly, giving poor Shannon a bit of a start, causing her to almost drop the scrambled eggs she had just whipped up.

Dangerous Secrets

Turning quickly, Shannon looked at Sam and replied "Well Hello to you too! You about scared the crap out of me. What's up with that?" Shannon now noticed Sam was holding the Album she had placed in the Den the night before. Shannon's eyes, fixed on the book, asked "So, where did you find that?" Sam told her it was on his nightstand by his bed when he woke up this morning. He was wondering how on earth it could have just showed up like that because it was not there when he went to bed. Shannon started to talk, "Strange, that's not where…" Shannon caught herself before finishing her statement and covered with, "Where I remember seeing it last. How on earth did it get on your nightstand form the den?"

Hoping she had covered herself from giving away that she knew about the book, Shannon was puzzled by where Sam said he found it. She knew she did not mistake his room for the den and did not go back to put it there later. "Well." Sam said continuing "It's the strangest thing then I guess. I had a dream about a photo Album and when I wake up, its right there, waiting for me." "Hmm, that is strange." Shannon responded, as Sam walked over and sat at the kitchen. He placed the book upon the table and then sat there, staring at it.

After a minute, Sam got up, telling Shannon, "I'll look at it later, I need finish getting dressed first. I'll be right back." While he was out of the kitchen, Shannon kept trying to figure out how that book could have gotten in Sam's room. It was a mystery for sure. Shannon went over to the book and opened it to see if it was the same one or not. Sure enough, it was the same one she had pulled out of the attic and set in the den to be found later that day.

As she closed the book back up, Sam re-entered the room, catching her just as she was closing it. "Find anything interesting in there?" Sam asked. "Oh, just took a peek is all. I haven't looked at one of the old albums in years." Shannon answered. Sam sat down and looked at the book, wondering why it was so important. As he slid it close to him, he remarked to Shannon. "I haven't looked in one either since a certain day. I suppose I should though and put some closer on all this. I mean, there's nothing wrong with keeping the memories going."

Shannon watched as Sam opened the book and started to look over all the pictures. First off, he saw one with Robin and himself standing in front of there home when it was done being built. Shannon could see a tear starting to from. Sam held it back however as he continued to look on. Next, there were some vacation pictures from the summer just before the accident. Shannon saw the look in Sam's eyes, the memories of happier days were starting to flood his mind. The look Shannon saw upon Sam's face was one of sudden loneliness and heartache.

◆

Sam closed the book before he totally lost it in front of Shannon. He was not ready for the memories the pictures brought back. Shannon wanted to say something as he started to close the book because she knew he not gotten to the pictures of Robin and her sister yet. Instead, Shannon kept her mouth shut though and walked over with Sam's breakfast, placing it in front of him. He told Shannon he wasn't very hungry right now. Shannon insisted he eat, saying it may help get his mind off of the pictures for a bit. She then asked if he would like her to put the book out of sight for now and he could look it over some more later, when he gets back from work. Sam agreed it was a good idea, pushing the book aside, toward Shannon to pick up. While eating, Shannon asked about the dream.

Sam was hesitant at first to tell her, but decided what the heck, why not? Sam told her about the boat, the night air, the sky. He talked about Robin and the Album she wanted him to look at. "There you go!" Shannon exclaimed "She put it there! Now you Have to look it all over and see if you can figure out what ever it was that she was talking about." Sam nodded, as if to say "Yeah, right!" looking at Shannon feeling she was the one who put it there and the dream was coincidence. Sam finished his meal, got up from the table to make a last minute check to assure he had everything he needed before leaving for work.

Grabbing his Briefcase, he then gave Shannon a little one-arm hug good bye before leaving. Shannon started to clear the table but was compelled to look at the album again. Before she could sit to open it up, the phone rang. "Hello?" Shannon answered. The voice on the other end was Kathy. She was of course looking for Sam. Shannon told her he left for work already. She wanted to say a lot more to Kathy, but not until Sam saw the picture first. It was so very hard for Shannon to keep her mouth shut and not say anything. As Shannon said good-bye, she did say something else as well. Shannon wanted to get the message across so bad that she knew who Kathy was. So with out really thinking about it,, she let it slip out, subtly, saying, "O.K. If you don't get hold of him at the office, I'll let him know you called when he gets home. Good-bye and have a nice day Ms. Vasure." Shannon hung up immediately after saying that, realizing what she had just let slip out.

Kathy sat speechless as she sat at the other end of the phone, now listening to dial tone. Kathy's last name was never mentioned at dinner last night, nor did she ever tell Sam of course. Kathy hung up the phone and though hard about what Sam must be thinking right now if he too knew who she really was. "Did Shannon say something to him or not?" was the number one thing on Kathy's mind right now.

A lot of ideas and thoughts went through Kathy's head in anticipation of talking to Sam again. "What will I say if he knows? What if he out right confronts me about it? How will I act? How will HE act?" Kathy realized that she was falling for him and didn't know what to do now. She didn't want to loose him, but how can she keep him now? Sooner or later she would have had to tell him anyway. Kathy did not want him to be finding out this way. Not like this.

So then she thought, "If he does or doesn't know yet, I could tell him right off, the next time I talk to him. It will look more sincere that way, rather than letting him speak first and me then sounding like I'm just trying to talk fast in order to get out of trouble. Maybe he will even understand." Kathy shook her head a little as she then thought, "Maybe, He'll shoot me where I stand too!" Kathy had certainly set up a little dilemma now for herself and she knew it big time.

Chapter 25

Sam arrives at his office and parks quickly, his mind is not on work at all this morning. All the way up to his office, Sam thinks about the dream, the photo album, why is it so important? With so much on his mind, Sam walks into his office, going right past Rachael without saying a word. Rachael just looks at him walk on by. Concerned, she stands up, then follows him into his office. "Well Good Morning Sir!? Are things OK today?" She asks. 'Yeah, there OK, why?" Sam answers. "Well, it's just that in all the years I have been with you, you have never just walked on by without saying Good-morning. So…." Sam interrupts, quickly apologizing for not greeting her.

Rachael suggested he just go home and get some rest since there are no meetings or anything going on till the afternoon. Sam then sat down and told her again that he was O.K. Sam also told her a little about what was on his mind because of a dream he had last night. Rachael said ok and that she will keep things quiet for him so he can just rest in his office then. Rachael walks out of his office, closing the door behind her. As Sam leaned back in his chair to relax, Rachael buzzed him on the phone saying "I know I said I wouldn't bother you but Kathy is on line two and I thought you would want to talk to her." "Oh yes!" Sam said excitedly.

He picked up the phone and said Hello. Kathy was a little quiet and hesitant in her words, not knowing what to expect. Sam asked her if something was on her mind, Then jokingly said, "Seems a lot of that is going on these days." Kathy took a deep breath while trying to find a way to know if Sam knew or not about who she really is. "Well, I'm a little quiet cuz, you haven't said anything about last night yet. I'm sure you and Shannon talked. My ears were burning for hours." Kathy let out a little laugh as Sam answered back. "Actually, we didn't really talk much about you, other than that she though you were a nice lady. She seemed to not want to talk much on the ride home. Guess she was tired. We went to bed as soon we got home."

Kathy picked up on that last sentence, deciding to have some fun with it. "You two went straight to bed Huh? I've heard of taking good care of your Staff and giving them a Bonus but….." Kathy kept her voice calm and showed now sign of laughing at all. Sam quickly scrambled for the right words to let her know he didn't mean it that way. "Shannon and I are just Boss, Employee. We also happen to be friends as well. I've never slept with her or even came close." Quickly, Kathy said, "Relax, I'm joking around with you."

The reason Sam did not see the humor in this at first, was primarily do to the image of Shannon in the mirror the other day. Kathy's comment made Sam remember that image quickly, causing a feeling of guilt that he couldn't explain. They talked for a bit more before deciding to meet for lunch. Kathy told him she had something very important to tell him, but had to do it in person. Sam agreed and set up a 1pm lunch at the local restaurant where they had been before. Kristy entered the room as Kathy hung up the phone. "So, I hear you are going to tell him something HUH? Perhaps your real last name?"

Kathy looked directly at Kristy, she didn't like the tone Kristy was using at all. "What I tell him is what I tell him. Why are you being so, so, insistent on this?" Kathy asked. "Well" Kristy started "I care about you and your feelings. Who knows what may happen to you with what you are trying to do. I watch the news, I read the paper, I know about people disappearing after messing with a corporate big wig." "Oh Please" Kathy said "I think you've been watching too many crime dramas. I know what I am doing. I also DO really appreciate your concern. But you know me, always got an angle and a way out."

Kathy then stepped close to Kristy and gave her a big hug to reassure her things will be fine. Just then, Adam walks in and sees the hug. "Wait,

wait, I'll get the video cam before you go any farther!" Kathy started to laugh as Adam turned around like he was really going to get the camera. Kristy piped up with "Oh get real!" "Yeah!" Kathy added "Kristy is way too short for me anyway." The two ladies laughed as did Adam. "So, are you going to call Shannon today for lunch, maybe?" Kristy asked. "I was thinking about it. Kathy, you have Sam's home number?" Adam replied.

Kathy was unsure of letting anyone talk to Shannon till she got a shot at Sam. "Sure, what time you thinking of going?" Kathy asked. Adam told her that would take his usual lunch time from work around 1 ish. Kathy figured 1 would be good because she would already be talking to Sam at that time. Kathy wrote down the number and handed it to Adam, who then left to the other room and called the number. After 4 rings, Shannon answered "Hello! Mr. Katz residence, may I help you?" Adam smiled when he herd Shannon's voice "Yes you can my lady. I am in need of a lunch partner for this afternoon and I could think of no one else I would rather have lunch with than you." Adam responded.

Shannon paused for a moment, to think before responding because she didn't recognize who the caller was. "Oh, I see. And you pulled my name out of a hat? Or maybe looked through a phone book for rich guys who might have a housekeepper?" Adam got a little embarrassed on his end of the phone. "I'm sorry, this is Adam, from last night? I should have said that first. Thanks for not hanging up on me." Adam quickly said. Shannon giggled and answered "Oh I wouldn't have hung up. A girl has to keep her options open ya know. I do have a few things to do today but what time were you thinking of?" Adam was relived to hear her say she would. "Well, I figured around 1 at that little restaurant on the corner, off Main Street."

Shannon thought about it, then told him she had not been there in ages and that it would be a great place to meet. The time and place were now set and Adam said good bye. A little past 11, Sam came home like he does often for lunch. "Hello, home for lunch?" Shannon exclaimed. "No, I'm having lunch with Kathy today so I won't be eating here. Also, I just couldn't wait any more, I had to look at the album. I just can't get it off of my mind." Sam told her.

Shannon was almost speechless from what she heard Sam say. "You're….. going to look at the book and then see her huh? Why get yourself all worked up and then be no fun at all when you meet Kathy? I think you can wait till after and then look." Shannon said, hoping Sam would take her advise. "Nope, gotta look now. It's been long enough, I can handle it." Sam said as he sat down at the table where the book still laid. Again he opened it and went page by page. This time, his mind was on what Robin said to him the dream.

"Just what was it though," Sam though "That could be so bad and terrible?" After a few pages, Sam's eyes opened wide, he thought his heart was going to stop when he came across a certain picture. He stared, not breathing at all for a moment. Shannon was keeping an eye on him while he went through the album. Shannon noticed right away then when he came to the picture. Quickly, she walked over and said "Sam, Breath! Tell me what's wrong!" Sam could not say a word as he just turned the book toward Shannon and pointed. Sam had found the picture of Robin and Kathy standing together.

Shannon knew she had to act surprised "Oh My God! It's Kathy? But, why didn't she tell you? I mean…" Sam, with a very sad and upset voice cut in "Because she's playing me for a fool! That's why. She wants something. So that why on our first date, she kept asking about AMTRON, now I know. WHY? Why didn't I see this?" Sam was seeing red and wanted to confront Kathy right now, not waiting till 1 for lunch. Shannon put her hand on Sam's shoulder to help comfort him, standing there beside him, not saying a word.

Shannon wanted to say just the right thing to help Sam through this. Shannon could think of nothing right away. Sam spoke again before Shannon said anything. "You said you thought she looked familiar and even Rachael said she sounded like Robin. But Nooooo, I couldn't listen, I couldn't…" Shannon quickly interrupted before Sam beat himself up any more. Still not knowing what to say though really, Shannon just spoke from her heart. "Now Sam, Things will work out, you'll see. Maybe she just didn't want to get involved with her sister's husband. Perhaps she just wanted to get to know you a little better first and….." "Yeah right!" Sam exclaimed "She told me a fake name in the beginning and then another one and who knows what else she has lied about. No, I'm going to get to the bottom of this and tell her a thing or two."

Shannon's heart was breaking over the way Sam had been so hurt. "Sam, Please! Calm down first. I have an idea for you. Please, listen to me."

Shannon pulled up a chair real close to Sam and took his hands in hers. She looked him right in the eye and then continued. "Take this picture with you to lunch. Don't look mad and just put on good fake smile, like you do at most of your board meetings with investors." Shannon saw the slightest hint of a smile breaking though, she knew she was helping. "Then, after you sit down with her, tell her you have a little something for her that you thought she might want to have as a keepsake. Pull the picture out casually and place it in front of her. Then, let her squirm, while you play it like a hostile take over."

Sam thought for a moment, then looked at the picture again and then back at Shannon. "I really don't know how I would manage without you Darlin" Sam said as he reached out to give Shannon a big hug. Shannon held back the tears, feeling she needed to be strong for Sam and show things will be fine. Sam got up and went to the bathroom to freshen up a bit before going to meet Ms. Kathy. Shannon really wanted to be there when Sam drops that picture on her, so she could be there to pick Sam's heart up off the floor. Shannon also couldn't break her lunch date or Adam may think something is going on.

After she thought that, it hit her. Shannon became very angry. Like Sam, her eyes were seeing red now as she thought about Adam, "That Bastard! I'll bet he knew all about this since Kathy lives there and they are all old buddies. Just wait till I see him, just wait!"

Chapter 26

Tucking the picture neatly in his pocket, Sam took it with him to go meet up with Kathy. All the way to the restaurant, he kept thinking about what he would say to her and how he would act. Sam's heart was broke into a million pieces. Then, he remembered the dream and what Robin had told him about forgiving her. "What does her sister have to do with forgiving her?" Sam thought to himself. Realizing there must be more to this story, Sam decided to keep a calm head. Before he knew it, he had arrived at the restaurant where Kathy was waiting for him.

    He could see her through the window, waiting for him. Kathy was at the same table they had the first time they went there. "How cute." Sam thought sarcastically. As he approached the table, Kathy got up for hug, greeting Sam with a little smile. Kathy could tell by Sam's look on his face and the half hearted hug that something was not right. She decided to get right to the heart of the matter and spill it all. Before she got two words out, Sam interrupted "I came across something for that I thought you might want to keep in a scrap book or something. You know, for the memories." Kathy was a little confused as Sam reached into his coat and pulled out what looked like a picture. With a casual flick of his wrist, Sam let the picture drop right in front of her.

    Kathy's eyes turned away quickly after realizing what the picture was. Then, a tear started to from. Kathy held it back by taking a slow deep breath. She looked at Sam, then back at the picture, then back at Sam. No words were able to leave Kathy's lips as she tried and tried to speak. Finally she spoke, "I am so sorry Sam. I wanted to tell you at first, but decided to just keep quiet. I didn't…." Sam cut her off in mid sentence. "Didn't what? Want to blow your little scam on me to get information?" Sam was quite upset, but kept a calm tone and cool head.

"No." Kathy continued "I wanted to just do what I came here for and leave. I was going to tell you today when we got together and….." Again, Sam interrupted "Today? Yeah, maybe you were, maybe you weren't. Its all lies now as far as I see it." "You don't understand Sam, Please let me talk" Kathy pleaded. "Why? You took me for a fool and played me like a fiddle. I'm just pissed cuz I didn't see it coming and I should have known better. I've dealt with more hard core people than you and never got burned, so you can put that one in your book of records as the first ever to get one over on ol' Sammy boy! I'll bet that will be quite the little high spot for you Huh?" "Stop! Please Sam!" Kathy said not to quietly as she was letting the tears flow now and figured she had nothing to loose so why not just tell everything.

I didn't mean for any of this to happen this way. I actually am falling for you. I meant all the things I said to you the other night and….." Sam started to loose his temper as he listened to Kathy. "Look! How am I supposed to believe you after what you did? You lied to me from the beginning. I'm sorry you started to grow a heart now but I am not, nor will I, continue this with you. I just can't. Also, I hope you got what you came for cuz this information both is closed." Kathy took a deep breath and wiped the tears from her face. "OK. That's fair enough Sam" Kathy said. "But let me tell you the whole thing. The true chain of events whether you wish to believe me or not."

Sam thought for a moment and then figured it was the least she could do by telling him the truth, if it was going to be the truth. "OK, I'll listen." Sam said half heartedly as he concentrated his attention on what Kathy was about to say. While Kathy was about to speak, Adam walked in and sat down to wait for Shannon. Adam saw Kathy sitting over on the patio area and could tell it was tense moment right now and did not want to interrupt. Soon, Shannon arrived and joined Adam at his table. Adam could tell Shannon was a little fit to be tied right now and the look on her face was not a good one.

"Umm, whats up?" Adam said in hopes to hear she only had a bad day so far and he was not in some kind of trouble already. Shannon looked him right in the eye and asked, "So, When were you going to tell me? Or were you in on the whole scam as well? Didn't Sam give enough info on what ever Robin's little sister wanted?" After saying that, she sat and smiled real big at Adam. Shannon quite enjoyed watching him twitch in his seat, trying to think of an answer. "I, Umm, figured that was between Kathy and Sam. I had nothing to do with it. Nothing at all. Honest!" Shannon sat there, wondering if she should believe him or not. After all, it is possible he was just a by stander in a way, Shannon thought to herself.

Shannon looked at Adam and saw this as her way out, she really didn't want to be dating him anyway. "Ya know." Shannon started "I really think this is a mistake. One big mistake. If you think I'm going to start something up with you then you need to think again. No-One messes with my Sam for any reason." Shannon then got up to leave. As she started to walk to the door, she noticed Sam and Kathy sitting at their table. At first, Shannon wanted run on over and deck the bitch, but instead, she held back. Shannon decided to sit at the bar and try to listen instead.

Adam saw her sit back down so he got up and came over. He hopped to explain, but before he could say anything, Shannon whispered to shut up and sit down. Adam did as instructed as Shannon motioned to Sam and Kathy, sitting not too far away. Shannon could hear Kathy's story quiet well. "And that's what lead up to all of this." She heard Kathy say "So, since Bill was trying to black mail Robin, by telling you they were having an affair and the stock was a love present for services rendered. All Robin had to do was actually sleep with bill and he would never say anything. Just one night, that's all. Robin would have nothing to with it though. She only wanted to buy a little stock at a time till she became a major stock holder, then, surprise you with it one day." Sam interrupted "What? How would her being a stockholder in another company that's my completion, make me happy?" Sam waited for an answer, as so did Shannon listening in. "Sam" Kathy continued "She bought the stock for YOU. This way you and her could control the competition. Don't you see? The plan backfired though. She never intended to go through with it, but let Bill believe she was. Of course Bill started to get impatient and became a bit on the aggressive side. As you know, our Robin was no fool and had to figure a way out as to not loose you and not have to sleep with Bill. She loved you Sam, with all her heart and soul.

Sam spoke as Kathy took a slight pause to gather her thoughts and continue. "Well then tell me this, if Bill was going to try something to get his way with her then why kill her? That got him nothing. Your story is not panning out here." "Let me finish" Kathy said "The only way Robin knew to put an end to all this was to take Bill out of the picture. That little stray rocket was meant for HIM not her. I didn't know it went all wrong till months later when I had not heard from her. I figured if things didn't go right she would have been calling me right away. I did some checking and found what had happened. I started my own plan then to bring Bill down. And yes, I was going to keep it for myself. Problem is though, I let my heart intervene and now I don't really care about Bill, just you."

"Well, that really does sound good." Sam replied "But tell me this then. Why did you not call me to find out what happened and why so long to come over and do what ever it is you are planning?" As Kathy thought for a moment, Shannon could take no more and stood quickly. Boldly walking to Sam's table she remarked "Yeah, I would Love to hear this one myself." Not even realizing or thinking what Sam may think of her barging in like that. Adam stayed back a bit and watched. Kathy looked at Shannon with a start and very surprised look on her face.

Kathy was very mad over the intrusion and stood up to face Shannon. "I'm talking to Sam, not you. Shouldn't you being washing something or cleaning?" Shannon's temper grew hotter as she replied "Look Bitch, I'm going to wash you in a minute here if you…." Sam quickly got up from the tabled and loudly called Shannon's name. Shannon stopped short of her whole sentence, looking at Sam. Shannon knew she probably should have kept her mouth shut, but just couldn't. Looking at Sam, Shannon started to say "Well, you aren't saying anything so I…." Sam sternly looked back at her, cutting her off by saying, "Shannon!? I told you I would handle this and I meant it. I do appreciate very much your coming in like the Calvary, but I can and will handle this my way. Now, please, go home and we'll talk later." "But…you…." Was all Shannon could say as she saw that Sam was never more serious in his life. The cold stare he gave was enough to shut her up.

With attitude to spear, Shannon looked at Kathy, softly saying with teeth clenched, "You're not Robin!" Sam took deep breath and looked at Shannon. Shannon looked back at Sam and quickly said, "OK! I'm going." Shannon turned and walked right on past Adam with out even a glance. Sam Watched as Shannon left, bringing attention to seeing that Adam was there as well. Sam motioned for him to come over. He wanted to see if Adam wanted to add something to all this or not.

Adam just waved a little, pretending he didn't hear what Sam just said. He did not want to get involved at all. So rather than sticking around for the rest of the show, Adam turned and left the restaurant. Shannon, fumed all the way home. She felt that she should have stayed, regardless off what Sam had to say about it. Shannon had to leave though because of her biggest fear. She feared that if she didn't, she would be fired. This would mean not being able to see or be with Sam any more if she had to leave. At the restaurant, Sam sat back down and so did Kathy. There was moment of silence as the two wondered where to go from here.

Sam broke the silence and started to talk first, "Well, I guess I'm going to go home now and just think for a bit. Don't call me though, I'll call you when I sort a few things out." Kathy agreed and reached out for Sam's hand, hoping he would take it as a truce and know she was sincere, meaning all she had said to him. Sam pulled his hand away as she started to reach for it. As Sam stood to leave, Kathy looked up at him, saying with tears in her eyes "She was my sister ya know. I loved her too and did what I felt I had to. Please understand that Sam, Please?" Sam looked at her and softy said "Yeah. I know." Then walked away, leaving Kathy to sit alone at the table.

As soon as Sam left the building, her estranged partner in the white car came up and sat down. Kathy looked at him and just shook her head a bit saying, "I really don't have time for you right now." Oh really?" he said. "I heard what you were telling Sam and I have one question for you. Do you know what will happen to you if you double cross me?" Kathy looked straight at him and with a cold stare, looked him in the eye, saying "Look John, it was MY sister that got killed and I don't care if you've worked for Sam all your life and feel like you got screwed over." Kathy stopped there and paused for a moment, giving John time to interject.

"Yeah, O.K.!" John said and then added "Just remember, it was ME that tipped you off to the buy out. If I wouldn't have intercepted your call to Sam on that day, you wouldn't be getting your revenge on Bill. Now, when can I expect the figures on the bid?" Kathy took a deep breath as if she were thinking about his question. "Well, Bill said it would be tricky but I would get a copy soon. When I do, I'll give you what you need." Kathy got up from the table and turned to head out. John quickly stood, grabbing her arm to say one last thing to her. Before the words left his lips though, Kathy had a good hold of the gun she was carrying and let John know. Kathy quickly spoke, "Grab me again and you won't need to worry about any figures or your career either!"

John let go, saying nothing. He watched as Kathy walked away and went to her car. John sat back down, wondering what Kathy could be up to. "Something didn't sit right with all this." John thought to himself. "The original plan to take down Bill and get his company some how seemed to not be the main thing on Kathy's mind any more." John then reflected back even farther, to the day he met Sam and all the empty promises he felt that were made. John thought about the day he sat outside Bill's office. He was waiting to see Bill about some contracts Sam wanted looked over. The contracts were sort of a partnership agreement on the over all Federal contract that was split between them.

However, John waited, he over heard Bill's conversation to Robin on the phone about a little romp in the hay. John had never mentioned any of this to Sam though. Since the accident, he figured he could use that for personal gain and finally get ahead in his career. Bill wouldn't listen though to John's little black mail attempt. Bill just laughed and said he had no proof to get the Hell out of his office. John sat for an hour at that table, thinking and wondering.

Chapter 27

When Shannon arrived home, she walked in and saw the Album, still laying on the table. The book sat there and sort of stared right at her. Shannon felt compelled to open it and look one more time. As she did, memories from each picture danced in her mind. She remembered happier days when Robin was still alive. This time, Shannon went past the page where she found the picture of Robin and Kathy, looking now at every page in the album. As she turn the last page and looked, she rested her hand on the inside cover.

As Shannon looked over the last picture, her hand slid down the hard cover of the album. "What the?" Shannon thought to herself as her fingers sensed a small rise from under the felt backing. Upon closer inspection, Shannon noticed that one corner of the felt had been carefully taped back in place. Carefully, Shannon pulled back the tape and with two fingers, managed to push out the object underneath. To her surprise, it was a computer disc. It had no markings or labeling on it at all.

Being ever so curious now, as to what was on the disc, Shannon quickly closed the book and went up to her room. She could not get the disc in her computer fast enough to settle her curious mind. There was only one file on it, it was named "Robins Revenge". Shannon quickly opened it, seeing a great number of Files. She sat there opening one after the other, reading each one carefully. Shannon learned the whole ugly truth about Bill and his little wishes for play time with Robin. The documents revealed how after Bill turned down Sam's offer, Robin set up her own little take over, because her one goal in life, was to make Sam happy. Robin knew the take over and putting Bill out of business would bring a smile to her husband's face.

Shannon kept reading, hoping Sam would not get home and interrupt her, or worse, walk in and catch her. Shannon's eye's grew large as she read about the shares Robin bought and how Bill gave her such good, under the table deals, on them. Robin did lead Bill on a bit, giving him the feeling that perhaps something more could come out of this little new found friendship with Sam's wife. Bill talked about a few different secrets as to how his company handles things and how much he wanted her to leave Sam and be with him instead.

Through all the things she read, Shannon had to smile though when she about to read the last one. She noticed that at no time, in any of these documents, did Shannon ever see the words, I Love You Bill. She did see in a few where Bill said that to Robin, but it was never responded to by Robin. Robin played Bill well and collected enough information to bring him to his knees. Then wouldn't Sam be proud of his little wife. There was even mention of a few meetings between Robin and Bill. Robin documented everything, she was very clever in how she handled it all. Shannon sat there thinking, "You go Girl."

After actually reading the last one though, it brought a tear to her eye, as well as a few questions to mind. The last document was one that read like a diary of events, in her own words, sort of a collections of all the separate ones put together. Toward the end of that last document, it went on and on about how Bill was pushing her, wanting more than just friends, threatening to tell Sam everything if she didn't sleep with him.

In Robin's words, in the last paragraph, it read "I do not really wish to end things the way I am thinking of. I love Sam so much and with all my heart, yet I know what I must do. I didn't plan on things going quite this way but Bill gives me no choice. I will not sleep with that disgusting man nor give him the satisfaction of trying to ruin my marriage. I know clearly what must be done and done quickly. The 4th of July celebration is coming up soon, I just hope I can get hold of my sister."

It ended with instructions at the bottom, they read "If anyone ever reads all this stuff, then things did not go as planned. I may be in jail or

Dangerous Secrets

I may be dead. If it's not you Sam, reading this, Then Please tell him that I love him and always will. Also that I will keep him always with in my heart as I hope I will always stay with in his. I do know one thing though, if this whole thing goes wrong, and I do die, my last thought will have been of him, the most wonderful and loving husband in the world, SAM!

The document did not giving any details as to what she was going to do. Shannon wiped the tears from her eyes. She sat there, wondering if the accident that took her life really was an accident. Just then, Shannon Heard Sam's car. Pulling out the disc, she ran back to the kitchen with it. As Shannon managed almost have the disc back in, Sam entered the kitchen. Thinking quickly, Shannon pretended she had just found it. Sam asked what she was doing. So Shannon told him that she was looking over the pictures and came across something in the lining of the album. As Shannon handed him the disc, Sam's hands became a little shaky.

"I wonder if this is what she told me about in the dream, To Forgive" Sam mumbled to himself. Shannon asked him to repeat what he said but Sam did not. He turned and went to the Den, to see what was on the disc. Sam tried to prepare himself for what ever it was he may find out. As he waited for the disc to open, he just stared at the computer, watching that little hour glass on the screen.

Sam swallowed hard as he thought to himself "Robin, no matter what, I forgive and still Love you so very much." The disc opened and hesitantly he clicked on the file. Sam just sat for a moment, staring at all the documents now before him. With a gentle but quick little click on his mouse, the first one opened. Sam spent the next hour in his den, with the door closed, not being to sure what to make out of all this. Half way through the documents, Sam's eyes started to tear up, realizing what his wife had been up to and wished she would have talked to him instead of trying to surprise him this way. Robin was in way over her head. If she would have only told him, she would still be alive today and in his arms safely.

As Sam read the last one, he felt a strong tug with in his heart, reading his wife's final words. Sam could not hold back the tears or the feeling with in his heart as he stared at the last sentence. After a few moments, he then shut down his Computer and took out the disc. He held it against his chest. Getting up slowly, he went over to the couch to lay down. As he laid there, still clutching the disc against his heart, Sam pictured Robin's smile. Sam would have sworn that at that very moment, he heard Robin's loving voice once more, saying "I will always Love You Sam!" Sam laid on the couch, slow deep breathing, his only thought was "I DO forgive you my love, but Why Robin,,, Why didn't you tell me? I still love you so much and yes I keep you safe in my heart"

After a few more moments, Sam heard a soft knock on the door but ignored it. Another knock followed, still with no reply. The door then slowly opened. Sam ignored it all. It was Shannon, peeking in to see if Sam was OK. When she saw him laying on the couch, She quietly re-closed the door. There, Shannon stood. Knowing how Sam must be feeling right now. Knowing there is really nothing she can do to ease the pain or settle the thoughts he is having. Shannon quietly wept as she went to her room, leaving her door wide open in case Sam should call for her.

The phone started to ring, Shannon answered it quickly so as not to disturb Sam. The caller of course was Kathy. Shannon could tell she had been crying when she asked to speak to Sam in a shaky voice, accompanied by a few covered up sniffles. Shannon's first instinct was to tell Kathy off real good and slam down the phone, but she had to think of Sam right now and he might get mad her if she did that. Instead, Shannon talked in a normal tone and asked, "Haven't you done enough already Dear?" Kathy paused, then replied, "I deserve that and you're right, I've messed him up and I want to make things right though." Well." Shannon continued "He is not taking calls right now and is resting in the den. I'll let him know you called."

"I really am sorry…(click)…. For everything" Shannon hung up before letting Kathy finish what she was saying. Sadly, as Kathy hung up the phone, she realized that she may not ever again see or speak to Sam. For the first time in Kathy's life, she was now thinking of someone else for a change. She also knew that she could not be upset with Sam if he wanted nothing to do with her any longer. After all, she did lead him on in the beginning and lied almost the entire way through all of this. As Kathy mentally beat herself up over her situation, Kristy came home from work early. She walked in and saw Kathy, sitting on a chair in the corner of the living room, just staring off into space.

At first, Kristy wasn't sure if Kathy was even breathing let a lone awake. As Kristy walked over, she called out Kathy's name. Kathy did not respond. Kristy shook Kathy's shoulder, saying her name once more. Snapping out of her little trance, Kathy now responded "What? Oh, you're home early. How were things at work today" Kathy was still thinking of Sam and the situation. Kristy could tell there was something deeply on her mind and asked if there was anything she wanted to talk about. Kathy really didn't want any I told You so's, so all she said was, "Not really. Just deep in thought about stuff is all. I'm fine" Kristy knew better than that but didn't want to push it. Kristy knew Kathy all to well and that she would talk when she was ready to.

As Kristy turned to walk away, Adam came into the house. He was mad and let Kathy know it, as he slammed the door behind him. Adam walked right up to Kathy and started to yell "This is all your fault ya know! Shannon may have liked me if you weren't playing this little game of yours to get what you want! You should have….." Kathy stood up quickly, looking Adam straight in the eye, cutting him off by saying "Yes. I know! Now, Leave me a lone!" Kathy then turned a bit, brushing against Adam as she walked off to her bedroom, slamming the door behind her.

Kristy, back hand Adam a good one, right across the arm, saying "What the Hell you doing? Can't you see she's upset? Are you Blind? You make it sound like she ruined a great thing between you and Shannon. Gesh, it was just one date!" Then, Kristy too pushed past and walked off. Adam stood there, trying to speak to Kristy as she walked off. "What? Wait! You were on my side yesterday about all this, what happened?" Kristy heard him and stopped dead in her tracks right at her bedroom door. Slowly turning, she looked at Adam and only said "Typical Man! You just don't get it do you!?" then entered her room, slamming the door in Adam's face.

Adam stood there, wondering what she meant by that little remark. He wondered if he should go talk to Kathy first, or talk to Kristy first, or. Just stay out of it for now and go make a sandwich. Adam's stomach won this little internal battle, hands down. As He was in the kitchen, preparing a little something to eat, Kathy walked in. She had a very serious, yet far off look in her eye. She went to the Fridge and took out a soda, opened it and then sat at the table. Not a word was said from Kathy at all. When Adam finished making his sandwich, he too sat at the table quietly.

After a few moments, Adam said he was sorry for coming on so strong like that. It was just that Shannon was a real knock out and seemed to have a brain too. Now it looked as though the two would not be getting together any time soon and it was over before it even got a chance. Kathy looked up and softly told Adam that he was right in a way. After all this time, Kathy finally agreed that what she had done, was not done the right way. Adam listened as Kathy explained how she was going to simply get the bids, find out what one was the highest, change the one she had in there so it would be the highest and return the bids before anyone would notice them missing.

Adam was quite surprised at how cloak and dagger this whole thing had become. He was also surprised over the fact that all she was thinking about now was poor Sam and giving HIM the company instead of originally planned. Adam did show caring though, since Kathy did seem genuinely sorry for doing all this. Adam started to think that perhaps Kathy was in deed growing a heart after all. The phone started to ring, Adam got up to answer it and the person asked for Kathy. Kathy thought sure it was going to be John, bugging her again about the papers.

As Kathy said Hello, she heard a familiar voice on the other end. It was Bill. "Just wanted you to know that I have the certain something you are looking for. Meet me at the Casa Blanca at 11 tonight." Bill told her. Kathy, still upset over the days events so far only said "Ok fine. I'll be there." then hung up the phone. Adam asked who it was what he wanted. Kathy told him, with a solemn look upon her face, "That was Bill, he wants to meet and thus the final card will be played."

Chapter 28

Kathy went to tell Kristy about her meeting with Bill tonight. "I'm going to go and meet with Bill tonight and I wanted you to know in case something goes wrong." "What? Are you crazy? You can't go there alone. I'll go with you, Adam too for that mater." Kristy insisted. Kathy tried to explain that if there are other people around then Bill may just leave and call off the whole thing. Kristy thought that would be just fine, forget the whole thing and walk away. "You don't understand" Kathy told her, "I have to see this through and that's all there is to it." "Fine!" Kristy snapped "Adam and I will wait off to the side so he won't see us, but we'll see him and not take our eyes off you for a second, no matter what."

Kathy thought for a moment, then finally agreed. Kristy left her room and went to the kitchen where Adam was still sitting. "Did Kathy tell you what she is doing tonight?" Kristy asked. "Nope, just told me it was Bill and walked off to your room. Why?" Kristy told Adam about Kathy's meeting and that she felt her and Adam should be there to watch over it all. At first Adam was very against the entire idea. After all, he already lost out on a good lady, there's no telling what may happen at that little set up tonight.

Kristy did convince Adam to go though after pointing out that Kathy is like family and should be treated as such. "Besides." Kristy said, "How would you feel if something did happen and you weren't there to stop it? You know you like Kathy just as much as I do so we are going." Adam thought for a moment, seeing that he was not going to get out of this. "Fine, Sis! You win this one." Adam said, "But if something does happen, you sit and I'll go over to her." Kristy agreed.

When it came time to leave, Adam and Kristy went in one car and Kathy took her rental. That way, if seen arriving, Bill would not know there was a back up watching them. Kathy arrived first and parked. Right behind her, were Adam and Kristy. Kathy didn't even look in their direction as she got out and walked up to the meeting place. Bill was already there, waiting in a booth off to the right of the bar. It was dark in that corner and Kathy wouldn't have seen him if the bartender hadn't immediately asked her name and then said her friend was waiting there.

Lucky for Kristy, she saw where Kathy had gone to or they would not have been able to look after her. Adam and Kristy sat at the Bar while Kathy talked with Bill. "So? Where's the stuff?" Kathy asked demandingly. "Now now," Bill said. "First things first. You have to get these back to me by noon tomorrow so I can slip them back in before the opening at 2. That way no one will know they are missing. Now, if you get caught with these, I know nothing about it. Understand?" Kathy agreed and Bill handed over the bids. Casually she slipped them in her large handbag and stood up to leave.

All of a sudden, Kathy heard from the Bar, "Hey Sam! How's it going?" Total fear ran through Kathy's body as she managed to move quickly and sit back down, hoping Sam would not pick this side of the bar to sit. The voice that said Hello was Kristy, so, lucky for Kathy, Kristy talked and nudged Sam to the other side of the bar to sit, with out Sam realizing she was doing so. Bill too was a bit tense right now and wasn't sure what to do. His first thought was to grab the bids and run. Kathy was sitting low in her seat though so there was no way Bill could grab them away from her. Bill watched as Sam sat on the other side of the Bar.

Bill thought it to be quite lucky that someone was there that knew Sam and directed him away form this side of the bar. Bill didn't even think for a second that the person was there to actually be watching him and Kathy.

Kristy was doing a good job of keeping Sam's attention, enough to finally allow Bill to slip out quietly, unseen.

"Coward!" Kathy thought to herself. With Bill being gone right now, Kathy came up with a plan. She called the waiter over and told him to give Sam another of what ever he was drinking and she would pay for it. Also, to tell Sam it was from an admirer. The waiter did as asked and of course Sam was insistent on knowing who this person was so he could thank them. Kathy heard Sam asking and decided to get up now and walk on over. She had the whole thing figured out. "If things go according to what I feel he'll say to me, then I'll be out of here quick!" Kathy said to herself before walking over.

"Hello Sam, I was hoping you would be here tonight." Kathy said, not looking him straight in the eye but a little down at the table. "Well, Kathy, I figured you wouldn't be far behind since Kristy is here and…. Isn't that Adam sitting at the bar as well?" Sam replied. Kristy quickly excused herself from Sam and went to sit with Adam. She didn't really want to be in the middle of this little fireworks display. Kristy couldn't quite make out what Kathy and Sam were saying, but tried real hard to listen with out looking too obvious. "I just wanted to try and explain things a little is all and…."Kathy started and then was interrupted by Sam. "And what? You thought I would just forgive and forget? You send your little friends over to test the waters first?" Sam's tone was very cold, and so it should be after the little games Kathy was playing.

"No No, You have it all wrong." Kathy continued. "I deserve that remark, but I'm being honest here. Kristy and Adam insisted they come along in case there was a problem and I would need a shoulder. They really are good friends, so I really couldn't stop them. I was curious though and so I let Kristy talk to you first for a bit before I did anything. I wanted to make sure you would at least talk to me." Kathy took a pause, hoping Sam would say what she thought he would. Sure enough, Kathy heard the words come out of Sam's mouth. "I'm sorry Kathy but I have some thinking to do right now and so this is not a good time to talk. I do promise though, you will get your chance." When Kathy heard this, she felt relieved and yet hurt in a way, because he didn't want to talk.

Kathy knew she need to get with John right away now and finish his part in all this. Yet still, it would have been nice to see if she could settle things with Sam and perhaps get another chance. With a tear in her in eye, Kathy looked at Sam and said. "Ok, that's fair then. Please call me though when you wish to talk." Kathy waited for an answer as Sam took a deep breath before saying "OK, I'll do that. I promise." Taking a sip of his drink, Sam had nothing more to say. Kathy turned and walked out the door.

Kristy and Adam got up now too and were about to leave when Kristy told Adam to wait just a moment. She then walked over to Sam. Adam watched closely to see what Kristy was up too. Kristy went on over to tell Sam something before she left. "Sam?" Kristy asked "Just please hear me out and I'll leave." "OK, Shoot!" was Sam's reply. "Well, I just wanted you to know that I've known Kathy for some time now and I do know she is really sorry about this whole mess and if you just give her a chance to explain a bit more then…" Sam interrupted "Look, I told her I would call her later and I would listen. I have nothing more to say about this tonight so please, leave me alone and have a nice evening."

Kristy, having to have the last word, added "O.K. We'll go. I just wanted you to know she did not put us up to being her tonight and she is being 100% honest with you right now." To ensure the last word, Kristy turned with out waiting for a reply and signaled Adam to follow. Sam sat, shaking his head and thinking over all the events that have taken place. He thought about Bill and Robin, the dreams, the lies and under the table deals. He started to wonder if it was worth it now, putting Bill out of business because of something he thought was real and true. Sam didn't know what to think now as he finished his drink and ordered another.

On the way home, Kathy called John, to let him know she had the bids and needed to have them back by 11am the next day. this would give her time to meet with him, take care of his part of this and get back to Bill by noon. John agreed and said he could meet with Kathy early in the morning. After Kathy hung up, she pulled off the road and parked behind a building, out of sight of traffic. Carefully she opened the bids to see what the ranges were. Out of the 15 bids, Sam was in the lead with his offer being the highest. John's offer though, was at 4th place. Kathy knew what she must do. Quickly, she drove home. Getting there before Kristy and Adam, it was easy to go right to her room and get started, without being distracted or asked a bunch of questions.

Turning on her computer, Kathy took the cover page of Sam's bid and grabbed her digital camera. As the computer finished booting up, she took the camera and came in close, filling the camera's view with only Sam's page. A soft click was heard. Quickly, Kathy hooked the camera to her computer, loading the picture of the document. After a few cut and past techniques, Kathy changed the bid amount to read a few million less. This gave the appearance that John was not far off from Sam and would make it easy to out bid him. "But what about the other two bids that were higher than John's now?" Kathy thought to herself.

After a little more thought, she decided to change them as well. A few hours later, Kathy was ready to print out everything she had changed. Carefully, Kathy removed the staples, placing the new, fake cover sheet on top. In the morning, before meeting with John, she would go and make copies of the rest of the pages for the bids she altered. This way, that packet would look complete and real. Kathy kept the original sheets separate and safe. Putting all the items back in the envelope, Kathy placed it by her computer for the next step in the morning.

As Kathy walked back to her bed to get some much needed rest and sleep, she accidentally knocked over her handbag. When it hit the floor, the picture Sam had given her earlier had fallen out. As she looked once again at the picture of her and her sister Robin, it seemed as if Robin was looking right at her. Kathy looked at the picture for a moment before picking it up. Sitting on the bed, Kathy starting to think of Robin and all the stuff they did when growing up. Kathy's thoughts soon came around to the night of July 4th, a few years ago, to the night Robin died. Holding the picture close to her chest, she said softly "I Love You Robin! Please forgive me." Kathy closed her eyes and drifted off to sleep, with the picture still in her hands.

Chapter 29

As the sun once more shined through the window, it hit Sam right in the face. Slowly, Sam turned from the light, placing his hand over his eyes. Shannon too, was a wake now. This time. As she walked down the hall way to the stairs, she noticed Sam's bedroom door was open. Taking a quick look inside, she saw he was no where in sight. Sam's bed wasn't even slept in. "That's strange" Shannon thought to herself. "He's never stayed out all night before with out letting me know. Maybe he left really early, because of the bid opening today? Of course that wouldn't explain his bed being made up." Shannon kept thinking about it until she walked down the stairs and past the den. As she went passed, she could her some familiar snoring going on in there.

Shannon peeked on in to see. Sure enough, there was Sam, sprawled out on the couch like someone had tossed him there as you would a rag doll. Shannon walked over and gently rubbed Sam's shoulder to wake him up. With a grumpy tone Sam said with his eyes still closed "What do you want now? Haven't you done enough damage already?" With that, Shannon spoke to him. "Excuse me? Damage? What are you talking about, Sam!?" Sam stretched a little, taking a deep breath and slowly opening his eyes. There was a blank look on his face as the vision of Shannon filtered through his cloudy mind.

Sam looked at her, one eye sort of shut, "Oh, it's you! Sorry, I thought it was someone else. Must have been dreaming." Sam then scratched his head a little, suddenly realizing he had slept in the den all night. Shannon asked what time he got home last night but Sam was not to sure about that. Sam was not to sure about a lot of things this morning. "Well." Shannon said "I'll have coffee ready in about 20 minutes. That should wake you up good" Shannon left Sam to sit on couch and wake up while she prepared the coffee.

Shannon did not recall hearing Sam coming home last night or she would have made sure he went to bed like she always does. She heard Sam yawn as he walked into the kitchen and then sit down at the table. She told him the coffee wasn't quit ready yet but Sam didn't respond. Then she asked if he was even going to go into work today. "What? Oh yeah, I'm, staying home today till the bid. I can't really concentrate right now till that whole deal is done. If someone needs me they know how to reach me. Coffee ready yet?" Sam finally said. Shannon looked at him and shook her head a little as she turn back around, facing the counter.

Mean while, Kathy wakes up and sees she has little time to get to the copy place before meeting with John. Seems Kathy over slept a bit. While she hurried to get dressed, Kristy walked in and tried to talk to her about the other night. She wanted to find out how it went with Sam since she couldn't hear anything from the bar. "Oh it went as I thought it would." Kathy remarked "He asked me to leave and so I did." "So what are you in such a hurry for?" Kristy also asked "I need to meet up with John and go over a few things and then get to Bill before noon." Kathy told her. Grabbing quick piece of toast, Kathy flew out the door and into her car. Hurriedly, Kathy made her way down the street.

"Dang!" Adam exclaimed "What was she in such a hurry about this morning. I didn't know that girl could move that fast." Kristy stood by the window looking out at Kathy as she drove off. "Well, seems she is all fired up to meet with that John fella and then get over to Bill for some reason. I just hope she knows what she is doing. This whole thing is getting a little bit much, if you ask me." Adam agreed and went back to reading his paper and drinking his coffee. Kristy stopped looking as Kathy turned the corner and was out of sight.

Arriving at a little out of the way place near the shore line, Kathy could see that John was already there, waiting for her. As Kathy parked, she took a deep breath and muttered "This it is. It's time." Kathy then got out of the car and walked up to John, sitting on a bench under a tree. "Good Morning Kathy!" John said with a smile. "I take it you have something to show me?" Kathy almost reluctantly handed over the papers, after she sat down. John opened them up very carefully as not to ruin the envelope. "Hmm, lets see now." John remarked as he went through each bid.

Something didn't look right to John though as he came to Sam's quote. "Now that's strange" he muttered to himself. "What? " Kathy said as she started to get nervous. "Sam must changed his mind on the amount. Figures though, Sam always was a bit on the cocky side when it came to business." Kathy was relieved to her what John said. Making Kathy feel quite confident, that she pulled it off. "Well, you know Sam!" she said with a light tone in her voice. John pulled out his revised copy. "I ran off 3 different amounts. Figured one of them would be high enough and if not, I'd just have to run home and print out another one." He said.

Kathy Looked cautiously as John matched up one that did go beyond the high bid. "Well, that should to do it! here you go, nice doing business with you Kat!" John said with a big smile as he resealed the envelope. As John handed it back to Kathy, he held on tightly as Kathy tried to take it. "Wait." John said "How about you and I getting together later and celebrate our little victory? We can have a good laugh over the look on Sam's face when he sees he didn't get the bid! Hahahahaha!!!! " Kathy remained calm, not saying what she first thought of John's offer. She'd rather shoot herself than spend time with John in the way he was talking about, or in anyway at all really. Kathy only wanted to get away and get through all this.

"Look, I won't be at the opening. I'm sure Sam wouldn't want me there. I also have things to do later so I'll call you and let you know if we can meet." Kathy replied. "Fair enough" John said. John then let go of the papers for Kathy to have back. He then walked with her to her car. Just before Kathy could get in, John reached over to steal a little kiss. She turned her head quickly so that all John got was the side of her cheek. John did not like this little stand off at all and let Kathy know. "You know, if it weren't for me, you wouldn't be here right now about to bring ol' Bill to his knees. I supplied you with all the information and times and dates. All you had do to was play your hand. And you did it quite well too. You get your satisfaction after all these years and so do I. And I would like a little bit of some other satisfaction too as long as you are here."

Kathy could not hold it in any longer. She tossed the papers inside the car on the passenger's seat and turned to face John. "Now look here, I'm grateful for helping me but not that grateful." John grabbed Kathy by the arms and yelled at her "No, YOU look here. I can take you down to ya know. So if I…." "If you what?" Kathy yelled back, interrupting John. John suddenly felt something pushing up between his legs. He looked down slowly, he now saw the little handgun Kathy had. It was pointed up right between his legs and her finger was on the trigger. Quickly, John let go and took a step back.

Kathy did not move. Only smiled and repeated "So, if you What!?" John was quite mad, but felt he better not push or call her bluff. "Fine!" John remarked "Have it your way. For now! But this ain't done yet." John then turned and walked off to his car. Kathy waited for him to leave first, so he wouldn't see which way she went when she left. Till now, John didn't know where exactly that Kathy was staying and she wanted to keep it that way. Hurrying home, Kathy thought about Sam and all she had done to him. For the first time ever, Kathy was genuinely upset for using someone like that.

As she pulled into the drive, Kathy noticed Kristy's car was not there. Kathy was happy about that, figuring she could just go in and put the actual cover sheets back on and get out with out anyone seeing her or asking questions as to what she was doing. Going in the house, she called out to see if they both were gone or what. There was no answer, giving Kathy a feeling of relief. Quickly, she went to her room and started to make the changes back to what it all was. All of them but John's of course. Kathy wasn't feeling as proud as she thought she would at this point. Perhaps because of falling for Sam, something that was not thought of in the original scope of things. Kathy went back out to her car and drove off to meet up with Bill.

As she pulled up to AMTRON, she saw Sam getting out of his car. "Now what the hell is he doing here? Great! I knew this was going to smooth." Kathy thought to herself. Not wanting to be seen, she pulled quickly into the first row of parking and stopped. Looking in her mirror, Kathy could see Sam as he entered the building. Once out of sight, she parked her car on the far side, away from Sam completely. Kathy waited in her car for an hour, but never saw Sam come back out. The time was getting close to noon, Kathy had to do something fast. But how will she get the papers back to Bill with Sam in there was the question on her mind right now.

Kathy did come up with a plan, hoping it would work. Walking into the building, her handbag clutched tightly, she walked right up to Bill's office and asked if he was in. Bill's secretary told Kathy that he was in a meeting right now, but she could wait if she wanted to. Kathy wanted to just blow off what she was told and walk on over to Bill's door. She decided not to, instead, she asked the secretary to have bill page her when he is done.

Kathy handed her the number and then left. She went down the hall and around the corner to wait. She had a good view of Bill's office from there and would see when Sam left. Finally, at 1pm, she saw Sam leave. It seemed to take forever for that Elevator to come so Sam could get in and leave already. When she heard the elevator doors open and then close, Kathy started on her way back to Bill's office.

Upon entering, she found Bill, standing by the secretaries desk as she was handing him Kathy's number. "Come on in." Bill said with a smile. Kathy walked on in and sat down in a hurry. Making sure no one was going to come in first, Kathy looked at the door and then back at Bill sitting behind his desk. "O.K. Here!" Kathy said as she handed back over the envelope that contained the bids. Bill commented as he grabbed the envelope and stood up. "You know, the board came by at 12:30 to pick these up. Luckily I was in a meeting already with your buddy Sam, so they said they would return at…."

Just then the secretary called Bill on the ICM. She announced that the guy from the Board was there to pick up the bids. Quickly, Bill said he would be right with them. Hurrying over to the Safe, Bill placed the envelope inside and closed it quietly. He then went to the door, to let the person in. Both walked straight over to the safe, while Kathy sat patiently, like she wasn't interested at all in what they were doing. Bill opened it up and then handed the envelope over. The Board member looked it over real quick, looking for, but not finding, any evidence of tampering. Upon seeing that all looked fine, the Gentleman smiled, saying Thank-you.

As the gentleman left, Bill went back to sit down. As he did, Bill let out a soft sigh of relief from how close that was. "Those boys sure are prompt, aren't' they?" Bill exclaimed. Kathy told him she would have had them here on time, but when she got here, Sam was already in his office, so she had to wait. Bill understood and didn't get upset at Kathy for being late. Kathy stood up, telling Bill "Well, I have nothing more to do here now or with you either. So I'll be going on my way then and remember this, I'll never forget what you caused and I hope you can sleep at night when this is all over. I'm sure I will. Good Day!" Kathy then turned to leave as she heard Bill say "Oh I'm sure our paths will cross again. Good day to you too!"

As Kathy left, she lightly slammed the door behind her, as one last little show of seriousness. Bill sat back down at his desk, looking over at his clock. He saw that it was time to get going, the meeting was a bout to begin that would determine now, the fate of many.

Chapter 30

As all the People arrived, each took there place at the table in the conference room. Soft muttering is heard. The one question that is on everyone's mind the most is, where's Sam. At the last minute, Sam enters the room and sits. The Board of director's for AMTRON were already calling the meeting to order. Bill then stood up to say a few words. "Thank-you all for coming, showing such an interest in my company. You know, it's not too late to just invest and get me back on my feet?" Bill smiled, hoping they would take that as light humor.

All the while though, Bill wondered what Kathy did with the documents to swing them in Sam's favor. Bill sat down as the Chairman took his place at the huge screen in the front of the room. He turned it on to display the list of Companies that were bidding. The envelope was opened, each name was called off with the amount of there offer. As each one was said out loud, the amounts appeared on the screen by their name. Sam was not paying too much attention though, he was pre-occupied, wondering why John was sitting there with a smile, across from him at the table.

John's name was called and the amount was listed, 19.5 million with Capital down of 2. John now looked over at Sam with a smug look on his face. John felt comfortable in his knowledge that he was about to get one over on Sam. A few more were listed. John started to get angry as he heard the amounts being called out were higher than his. As they came to the last name "Samuel Katz, H.K. Industries. 25 million with a capital of 7 down." John could not believe what he was hearing. Not only was Sam high bid but there were two others over his as well. He knew right off he was double crossed by Kathy and almost stood to say something about the figures.

John caught himself though and remained in his seat, stewing over his loss. This was supposed to be his break, John thought, and now it's all gone. John knew he would be fired for going against Sam like this. Sam sat, smiling over his victory. The question was asked to the group if anyone felt these amounts were debatable or if in deed this was their quotes. This was asked to give validity to the security of the documents. Though John wanted to say something he remained silent.

As the announcement was given, that company would become the property of H.K. Industries, currently owned by Samuel H. Kates, the group applauded. Sam stood to go up front and sign the finally papers that would now make his years of planning finally pay off. For some reason though, Sam didn't have the feeling he thought he would once he put Bill out. So much had happened in the last couple of weeks that it made the victory seem not as grand.

When the meeting was over and everyone was leaving, Sam quickly went over to John. "So, you bid why?" Sam waited for an answer as he noticed John fidget a little before talking. "I was just wanted a piece of something I could call my own. I figured as long as Bill was out, it wouldn't matter to you. You said a million times you didn't want the company, you just wanted Bill to be gone. I saw my shoot and took it." Sam cut in with a low soft tone, looking John straight in the eye. "You know, I could have you arrested for using inside information like that for personal gain? I just wonder WHY you didn't bid higher, since you knew what my amount was. That's why your story won't hold water, John. Some little set up went wrong on you today didn't it!? I want you and all your stuff out of my building by the end of the day!"

Sam was quite upset over this. The look in eyes was cold and the tone of his voice gave John a chill deep inside. For a moment, John thought Sam was going to do something, not just speak. Sam kept his cool though and some how held back the urge to deck John right there on the spot. John stood there as Sam walked away, knowing his carrier was over. John's thoughts turned towards Kathy. He wanted to make sure she would live to regret screwing him over like this. At least then he would have something smile about.

When Sam got in his car, he saw Kathy, sitting across the street in her car. Sam paid no real attention her as he drove off. Kathy watched and decided to follow. She had hoped he would speak to her, even if it was to tell her to go to Hell! At least she would be able to say her Good-bye. Sam noticed she was following. He wanted nothing to do with her, so he sped up a bit for her to take the hint. With one desperate move, Kathy changed lanes and floored it, passing Sam, then cutting him off. Sam swerved, barley missing her.

As the two cars came to a complete stop, Sam got out and went up to Kathy right away. "What the HELL do you think you are doing? Trying to get Amtron was not your ONLY plan!? You want to finish me off too?" Sam yelled. Kathy looked up and said, "Please Sam, Hear me out. I only ask 5 minutes of your time." "5 minutes?" Sam replied "5 minutes and you think you can explain all the stuff you have done? This is too good to pass up so yes, you have your 5 minutes. Meet me in the park." Kathy agreed and the two of them drove off to the park.

Sam sped ahead, getting there before Katy. He went to a bench and waited while Kathy arrived, parked and come on over to sit. Sam sat, a look of disbelief on his face that she could have anything at all to say that he would want to hear. Kathy sat next to him, holding back the feelings that wanted so desperately to come out. "I just wanted you to know that in the beginning, Yes, I did plan on using you for information only. But I quickly got to know you. I felt what my sister had seen in you. I know it was wrong but you have to believe me.." "Believe you?" Sam uttered "Believe someone that gave a false name, Lied to my face and who knows what all else? Yeah sure I will. We talked about all this before, have you nothing new to say?" Sam said coldly, with a very hurt tone in his voice.

Kathy continued. "I know I told you this before. You have every right not to believe me after what all has gone on but maybe one day you will. What I didn't tell you though, was, I LOVE YOU Sam. I never thought that would happen but it did. If I could take it all back, I would. I will always remember our little trip and never forget how much I hurt you. If you ever find it in your heart though to forgive me and just at least not hate me, please let me know. That's all I ask"

Sam could tell by her emotions that she was actually being honest and up front for a change. Even though he did still have some feelings for her through all of this, Sam still could not bring himself to forgive the hurt she had caused right now. "Maybe one day, who knows" Sam said "But your 5 minutes is up and I have things to do. Have a nice trip back!" Sam added, as he stood up to leave. Kathy wanted to grab him and hold on. Not letting him go, make him see what it could be like for the two of them. Kathy knew she had blown it however. She just sat, saying nothing as she watched Sam walk away. Perhaps walking away was for the better right now, she thought to herself. "Goodbye Sam! My sister really knows how to pick them." Kathy said quietly as Sam drove away out of sight.

Not much after Sam left, Kathy's cell phone rang. It was John and he did not sound too happy. Kathy hoped she could get off the island and not have to face him but why should this be any different that how everything has gone lately? Agreeing to meet with him, John's voice made her feel very uncomfortable and uneasy. After all, he did say before, that if she crossed him he would make her regret it. Kathy drove straight home in hopes Kristy or Adam would be there.

As Kathy went into the house she saw Adam sitting in the living room watching a little T.V. and Kristy was sitting in there too. Luckily, Adam was off today. She asked if she could speak to them for a moment. Though they had their differences, they were all friends, very good friends, that would be there if the other needed. As Kristy and Adam listened to Kathy's apology and that she told Sam everything, Kristy stood up and gave her a hug. Adam stayed seated, asking, "So, what do you want from us?"

Kristy wondered the same thing. Kathy asked if wanted them to come along, to keep an eye on her while John talked with her. Adam was not too sure about the idea of Kathy meeting with John at all. "This is sure to be trouble" Adam thought to himself. The two did agree to go though, taking separate cars to ensure not being seen together. Adam and Kristy got a good seat in the park where Kathy and John were supposed to meet. Kathy sat at the same bench she had sat at when she talked to Sam earlier.

Soon, John arrived. Kathy grew very nervous as John slowly walked toward her, wondering what he was going to say or what he may do! John said nothing as he sat with no expression on his. Kathy was almost shaking but managed to hold it, not letting John know she was a little afraid of what he might say or do.

Chapter 31

John was not happy and it showed as he stared to speak. "Well, Dear Kathy, I hope things turned out the way you planned, You little Bitch! Your little playing around here is over. I told you what will happen if you screwed with me, now get up and lets go! What I have to say is not for anyone but YOU." John stood up, grabbing Kathy's arm, pulling her to stand as well. Adam saw this and got ready to move quickly if needed. "You better let go!" Kathy warned him. "Yeah? Or what?" John said "Now shut up and come along" John turned to start walking while still holding on to Kathy. Kathy pulled back in resistance.

John did not get two steps before Adam walked up. Kristy was not far behind but did have her Cell phone ready to hit 911 if needed. Acting like just a passer by, Adam stopped and asked if there was problem here? "Seems the lady don't want to go with you mister. Perhaps you should let her go." Adam said sternly. John looked at him and replied "No, maybe YOU should go and keep your nose out of other people's business." Adam placed a hand on John's shoulder and repeated "I said you need to let her go!"

John looked at Adam's hand and then back at Adams face. John did let go of Kathy, but only to take a swing at Adam. Adam avoided the punch and grabbed John's other arm. Twisting it up and around, he spun John in his tracks. Adam quickly grabbed the back of John's head, throwing him down, face first into the bench. All the while, Adam held on to John's arm. John started to squirm but Adam had a good hold. Kathy quickly pulled out her gun and Adam shouted, "Kathy! No!"

It was just enough of a distraction to Adam that he loosened his grip enough for John to slip out. John jumped away and stood there, his lip was split wide open and bleeding. Kathy stood there, Pointing the gun at John's heart. "Yeah? What are ya waiting for? Go ahead, Pull the Damn trigger. See if I care. You've already cost me everything." John said out of desperation. Kathy stood there, her eyes transfixed. Kristy yelled too, for Kathy not to shoot but Kathy heard no one and responded with no reaction.

Kathy felt she had nothing to loose at this point so why not? After a moment complete silence by everyone, John made his move and grabbed for the gun. I single muffled shot was heard. Adam and Kristy stood in fright from the sound. John and Kathy stayed in their embrace, stared into each others eyes. Both fell to the ground as Adam rushed over. "KATHY!" Screamed Kristy with tear filled eyes. Adam pulled John away from Kathy, he saw the blood on both John and Kathy.

Kristy rushed over to Kathy, knelt down and held Kathy's head. Kathy was a bit stunned, but was still alive as Kristy kept saying "Talk to me Kathy, talk to me!" Adam noticed that John was not moving at all. He checked for a pulse but found none. Kathy looked over at John laying there. "I told you I don't miss." Kathy said with an unconcerned look in her eye. Kathy sat up, dropping the gun to the ground. She really didn't care what happened next. Adam grabbed the gun, placing it in John's hand. "Hey, I have a license for that you know, Give it back!" Kathy mumbled.

"Well, that ain't going to keep you out of jail. It will be easier to believe if his prints are on it as well, looking more like he attacked you." Kristy had already called 911. So with in moments, the Local authority arrives. Adam walked up to the officer, explaining, "We were sitting over there, when this guy comes up and grabs Kathy by the arm, saying to come with him. Kathy did not want to go so I stood up and confronted the him. He took a swing at me, but missed because I ducked. Next thing, Kathy grabs her purse and tries to leave. The guy grabs at her again, saying, "You're Dead Bitch!" Kathy dropped the purse to the ground. I grabbed hold of the guy who was still hanging on to Kathy and the three of us got into quit a little tussle. In the struggle, a gun was pulled. Kathy grabbed at it and suddenly it went off."

Adam kept his cool real good as the Cop asked a few more questions. The Cop could see the blood was on both parties, adding truth to the struggle part. He then looked at Adam and told him that he will be taking Kathy in anyway for questioning. "If everything is as you say it is, then she has nothing to worry about. She'll be let go. In the meantime though, I have to hold her" The Officer explained to Adam. He placed Kathy in the back of the squad. While the officer is now talking to Kristy, the coroner shows up, pictures are taken, then John's dead body is taken away.

Kathy stared out the window of the police car all the way to the station. The Gun was not registered so it could not be traced back to Kathy. Adam and Kristy followed in their own car. They went into the station and after a few hours of questioning, they were all released. The investigating Officers decided it was indeed an act of self defense. He also instructed the three of them to not be leaving the island for a few days, incase the D.A. wants to talk to them.

Chapter 32

Sam, of course, knew nothing about this little activity since he had driven straight home. Taking the rest of the day off, he wanted to think and try to clear his head. As he sat in his den, looking out at the pool, watching the water of move back and forth from the wind, Sam did manage to relax a bit. Shannon walked in, asking if there was anything she could do for him or get him. Sam did not respond. She then walked right in his view, asking again. "If I want something, I'll call you." Sam said before Shannon could finish her sentence for the second time.

Shannon said nothing at first as she turned to leave the room. She stopped at the door however, deciding enough was enough. Shannon turned back around, loudly saying "So, will you be feeling sorry for yourself the rest of the night or just till dinner?" "Excuse me!? "Sam exclaimed. Shannon had his attention now and continued "Well, seems to me like you would rather have this little pity party and see what YOU want to see. Not even think of or concern yourself with what's around you." "What are you talking about?" Sam said with a puzzled look upon his face.

Shannon walked closer, looked Sam right in the eye, "There people all over the world that loose a girlfriend's and wives. You need to get over it, like they did. Sure, it ain't easy but you have to." She also told him how since Robin's been gone he has done nothing but pour himself into his work and not really look around anymore. "You need to be strong!" Sam interrupted with "Now what would you know of the affairs of the heart and how it works, You don't even date!" Sam's words cut deep at Shannon's heart, causing her to break down and cry. Sam added "See, you're going to cry and you haven't lost anyone. Me, on the other hand, has lost more than once in that little game."

"Stop it! Just STOP IT already!" Shannon shouted. Sam took a step back, looking at Shannon in a way he had never seen before. He was not sure what to think at all. Sam's tone changed a bit as he spoke. "O.K. Calm down. We're both a little on edge here so,,,, why don't I take us both out for something to eat and just relax?" Sam told her. Shannon, breathing slow and deep as she said threw clenched teeth, "You really don't have a clue do you?" After saying that, Shannon just walked out of the Den.

Sam followed, trying to talk more. He caught up to her at her bedroom door. Asking nicely, Sam said "Shannon? Please stop. I'm sorry, Talk to me?" Shannon stopped and turned to him. The look on her face was that of heartache and heartbreak. Sam had never seen this before from Shannon. He walked up to her and asked again "Whats wrong, I know I shouldn't have said what I did. But I feel there is more to it, isn't there?" Again Shannon replied "You really just don't get it or see it do you? You walk around here feeling like the world has shut you out of being happy and with someone. That no one can be trusted and only want one thing from you."

Sam interrupted "Wait, you don't get my point at all, you are the one that doesn't see it for what it is. I have not met a woman yet that loved me for ME and not what I can do for them, accept for Robin. Guess having Money and power will only add up to one thing with women…." Shannon gave him a look to end all looks, as if daring him to finish that statement. It made Sam stop short of his full statement. After taking a slow deep breath, Shannon said "There women that care more for the Man's soul and heart than what's in his bank account. But you are just are too blind to see it! You'd rather condemn us all than take a chance".

Sam looked at her, seeing a side to her she never let him know about. He shook his head a little, then responded, "Yeah, sure there are. Not in the real world, at least not on This Island for sure!" With that statement,

Shannon started to cry and stepped into her room, slamming the door in Sam's face. Sam stood there for a moment and decided finally, "What the HELL, she's already mad at me." He decided to just boldly open her door and finish this. Sam noticed Shannon was on her bed, crying and mumbling to herself.

"So this is how YOU handle things? Don't seem to me like anything different that I do. I walk off too. So what do we do now? If this lady exists I would love to meet her but as I said….." Shannon rose from her bed, she pushed against Sam, telling him to just get out. She backed him up to the door but Sam would not leave. He wanted to finish this. "See? Why can't you just admit I'm right for ONCE, instead of always having it your way? Why"

Suddenly, something inside Shannon just snapped, The years of silence causing her to speak right over Sam's statement. "BECAUSE I'M A LADY THAT LOVES YOU FOR WHO YOU ARE AND NOT WHAT YOU HAVE!!" Shannon shouted. Sam lost all control of his words after hearing that. Shannon too could hardly believe she actually said that out loud to him. After a moment of awkward silence, Sam spoke softly and with feeling. "You what? You've never said anything before about this. You've always pushed for me to go out. I don't understand."

Shannon regained her composer, feeling like the world had just been lifted from her. Looking at Sam, almost seeming embarrassed of what she said, she answered "Well, I was never going to tell you because unless you felt the same then it would make things different and awkward between us. I decided I would rather have you the way it is than to have to leave and not see you at all. I know it sounds stupid, but I decided a long time ago that I would wait and if it never happened, then fine. At least I would get to live my life with you in it, in some way."

Sam didn't know what to say at all to what Shannon just told him. All he could do is look around a little as he held his hands together in front of him. Shannon looked down, gently placing her hand on his, continuing with, "Now, if you want me to train someone else to be your housekeeper I'll.." Sam's true feelings came out at last as he acted on impulse, stopping her in mid sentence saying, "Oh, you will definitely need to be training someone else to take your place around here." As Sam said this, he grabbed gently the sides of Shannon's face, tilting her head back. Without hesitation, Sam looked at her tear filled eyes and kissed her lips soft yet firmly.

Shannon looked at Sam, more puzzled than ever in her life. She asked "What? I don't understand. You kiss me and your letting me go?" Sam started to smile. Shannon asked what was so funny. Without letting go, he answered "Well, I am going to need someone to be taking care of this place if you and I are going to be doing things together you know." Wwwwhhat???" Shannon's eyes grew large, her heart started to pound hard and fast like a little kid at Christmas. She threw her arms around Sam's neck and Sam grabbed hold of her waste, picking her up from the floor.

Sam held her as he kicked the door shut. Walking over to the bed, he place her back upon the floor. Sam looked into Shannon's eyes, "You know, you are not the only one that has had a thought or two." Shannon's smile could not have grown bigger as all she said in response was "Oh really now. And you can prove this?" Shannon's hand reached behind Sam pulling him close. No words were said for the rest of the night. All that could be heard now, was the laughter of two hearts beating as one.

THE END